Unleashed Melody

Book 7

Dragonfly Cove Dog Park Series

Julie Carobini

Praise for Julie Carobini

"Fast-paced with unexpected twists. Carobini is a talented author and she uses her wit and charm to weave an enjoyable novel."
— *RT Book Reviews, review of Runaway Tide*

"So entertaining yet ... so deep and touches the depths of your soul! Bravo!"
— *B. P., review of Walking on Sea Glass*

"Captivating! Julie's books never disappoint."
— *Carol, review of Reunion in Saltwater Beach*

"This novel took me from my spring and dropped me into the heart of summer."
— *K.C., review of Chasing Valentino*

"A perfect holiday season escape."
— *Amanda Flower, USA Today Bestselling Author, review of A Christmas Thief*

"I continue to think about this story even after the last page is turned."
— *Anne, review of Windswept*

"Witty beach read ... hits the spot!"
— *Publisher's Weekly, review of Chocolate Beach*

Also by Julie Carobini

Julie's books are available in all your favorite stores, including her online shop: JulieCarobini.com

<u>Sea Glass Inn Novels</u>

Walking on Sea Glass (book 1)

Runaway Tide (book 2)

Windswept (book 3)

Beneath a Billion Stars (book 4)

A Sea Glass Christmas (book 5)

<u>Beach House Romances</u>

Beach Sunrise (book 1)

Beach Memories (book 2)

Beach Secrets (book 3)

Beach Sunset (book 4)

Beach Music (book 5)

<u>Standalone</u>

Reunion in Saltwater Beach

<u>Hollywood by the Sea Novels</u>

Chasing Valentino (book 1)

Finding Stardust (book 2)

<u>Otter Bay Novels</u>

Sweet Waters (book 1)

A Shore Thing (book 2)

Fade to Blue (book 3)

The Chocolate Series

Chocolate Beach (book 1)

Truffles by the Sea (book 2)

Mocha Sunrise (book 3)

Cottage Grove Cozy Mystery Novellas

The Christmas Thief (book 1)

The Christmas Killer (book 2)

The Christmas Heist (book 3)

Cottage Grove Mysteries (books 1-3)

Dedication

For my Labrador-loving friend, Debbie

Chapter One

Melody's eyes jolted from the text on her phone screen. Moving to the Sunshine State was supposed to cheer her up, not make her want to roll up her beach mat and hop a plane back to the dreary town where her ex had suddenly decided to run for mayor as if nothing heart-wrenching had ever happened between them.

She glanced at the text again:

> The boss wants to know why you're using
> the cherry plates for guests. It's on a Post-
> It … with an ! at the end.

Maria, her coworker, had sent the text while covering Melody's shift at the inn today. As the de facto manager of the Sunny Cove Inn, Melody hadn't counted on working Saturdays, nor had it occurred to her that the owner of the quaint bed and breakfast, Ethan Reed, would be AWOL, and instead, leave her sticky note missives to find first thing every morning. She hardly knew Ethan—he had spoken scant few words to her and her interview had only been by phone—but he made it clear in other ways that he was watching her from afar.

Melody sighed. She picked up her cell phone and let her thumbs fly across the touchscreen.

> I thought they'd be a nice touch. Feel free to go back to … paper.

> Sure thing, boss.

Maria added an emoji at the end of her text: a face with its tongue sticking out.

A laugh escaped Melody, followed by an unexpected lump in her throat. The swing of emotions lately had caught her by surprise. She was standing on the porch of a near-stranger's home on a balmy Saturday, and several people were coming up the walk behind her, all here for the same reason. The sun was glorious, yet her mind wandered back to a picture-perfect day back home. When she had loaded up her car in Ohio with two suitcases and one large chest of belongings, she never imagined that she would look back over her shoulder at this decision to move.

But ... even on the cloudiest of days in her hometown, she'd always find that old weeping willow by the creek to sit under and dream. At this moment, as she waited for the owner of the home's door to swing open, she missed the swaying branches and the dreaming.

A floorboard beneath her squeaked and she darted a look into the bright sky. A palm tree swayed. Melody pushed out a sigh and righted her shoulders, refocusing her attention on what lay ahead.

Long ago, she had made a promise to herself to say yes to adventure, and, for better or worse, she had kept her word. Still, as she stood on the porch of the local dog breeder's home, another thought began to push up through the soil of her mind: Was she ready for this?

"Mel! You're here!" Leslie flung open the screen door, her blonde hair tucked into a cap, and greeted her with a knowing smile.

"Did you have any doubts?"

Leslie laughed without answering the question. She acknowledged the others on the porch. "I'll be right with you all! Grab a notebook"—she gestured to a small stack on a table—"and I'll be back shortly."

Then she hooked her arm in Melody's and ushered her inside. "I promise you're not going to be sorry you came, my friend, not one bit!"

"I'm holding you to that."

Leslie gestured toward an open doorway that framed a frenetic jumble of cream-colored, fluffy activity. "Go ahead and say hello while I grab a new toy for your baby," she said, disappearing down the hall.

Melody slowed her steps and peeked into the room, which was a maze of gates and blankets and puppies piled onto each other, as if still in the womb. She tried to guess which one of the golden Labrador pups would be hers. When she'd let on to Maria, the only other soul she knew in town, that she was having second thoughts about adopting a puppy, the young woman advised her to pick the one that laid on its back and let her rub its belly. "That one will be teachable," Maria said.

But who would be there to teach Melody?

She took another step, and a trickle of sweat dripped down her neck. Was it the stuffy Florida weather or was this something else? *Please tell me this is not early menopause!*

She glanced toward the hall. She had only met Leslie a

couple of weeks after Melody moved to Dragonfly Cove to manage the inn.

Well, *manage* had become a rather loose term. She had answered the want ad in earnest and, with her mind made up to leave the Midwest, packed up her belongings and headed to Florida's Gulf Coast to start over with a new life.

It didn't take long for Melody to realize that Ethan still held a tight grip around the reins of the place, even if most of their communication was in writing. As a former operations manager of the largest hotel in Ridgburg, Ohio, she knew that a supervisory position for a small inn would require a different mindset, a slower one. And while she expected a learning curve of the inn's ways, she soon realized it would take some time and patience to coax the absentee owner into letting go a bit.

Melody still couldn't believe she had divulged her life story to poor Leslie the day she stopped by to drop off something for Ethan. A plant, was it?

After her time in the "confessional," when she had told the stranger too much about what had transpired in her world back home, Leslie had offered her a smile and some advice. "A new little being in your life will do you some good."

"Excuse me?"

Leslie threw back her head in laughter. "That look on your face! Classic."

"I'm sorry?"

Leslie's laughter faded to a genuine smile. "A puppy, I mean. Not a baby."

The pronouncement settled on her like a light blanket on a cool summer night. Leslie considered dog breeding a calling, she had told her as much that day. "Puppies are the sunshine of life," she said in a singsong voice. "They bring so much love to us, you know?"

Not really, no. Melody had nodded, but she hadn't really known that to be true personally. The reason? Melody had never had a dog.

As a child, her dad wouldn't allow it, and her mother had always been deathly afraid of them. Not to mention her best childhood friend, Stef. She let out a small sigh, remembering. Stef's family had a small dog that yapped at Melody every time she showed up to play.

"She knows you don't like her," Stef would always say over the dog's incredulous bark. "Start bringing liver treats so she won't bite your toes off."

Needless to say, Stef came over to *her* house more often than she went to her friend's.

Truth was, she may have faced various adventures head-on in the past to keep her ex's heart—parasailing in Catalina, ziplining in Punta Cana ... oh, and that last-minute whitewater rafting trip she took to the Ohiopyle—but she knew nothing about caring for an animal.

And yet, without much thought of what a puppy in her life would look like—*really* be like—she'd agreed. And that was that.

Leslie called out, startling her. "You ready to meet your new baby?" A hush of wistfulness laced her voice.

Melody exhaled. She glanced around again, second guessing everything. And then ...

"Here you are." Leslie swooped in, eyes crinkled at the corners, and, if Melody wasn't mistaken, they glimmered too. Ready or not, she placed a puppy in her arms.

Melody cradled the wiggly darling against her chest, marveling at the plushness of her buttery fur and the earthiness of her scent. The fear that she'd expected to spike made no appearance. Instead, the only unexpected emotion came from sudden tears. Not from despair, which had poked at her tender memories, but from something new. She could neither wipe away the smile nor stop the tears from coming down. *What is this?*

Just outside on the porch, excited chatter bounced around from those waiting to pick up their pup, but she was ... crying?

Leslie nodded with understanding. Though she didn't know her that well, apparently, the dog breeder extraordinaire could see right into her soul. If only Leslie could tell her how to put the patchwork of her life back together again ...

"Do you want to meet the other puppies before making a final decision?"

Melody startled and quirked her head in a question.

"There are four more to choose from," Leslie said, "in case you're not sure about this little lovey." She gave the puppy in Mel's arms several gentle strokes across her noggin followed by a quick kiss.

Melody shook her head, that swell in her chest growing larger still. "No, that won't be necessary. I've found my girl."

Leslie smiled and nodded, and Melody knew for sure now that she detected a shimmer in the woman's eyes, too. "I agree. I'm glad you've found each other, Mel." She paused. "What will you name her?"

Melody didn't hesitate. She hugged her new little friend closer and simply said, "Willow. I'm calling her Willow."

Chapter Two

The promise of a studio apartment to live in while she managed the inn drew Melody's interest in this sunny spot on the gulf from the start. It hadn't occurred to her that, no matter the time of day or night, she would feel a sense of being "on."

As in, always visible and available to nod a greeting, answer questions, and—the hardest for a late riser—chat. She'd have to tuck her chin down low and do her best to avoid making eye contact.

Sure enough, at 5:30 a.m., when she stepped outside in leggings, a tee shirt, and flip flops, she did a double take when her eyes caught a lovely couple strolling by in the shadows as if it were two-thirty in the afternoon. If she were back home, she likely wouldn't see a soul save for a delivery driver or two. But here in Dragonfly Cove, the weather would soon turn balmy—or balmier than it already was—so locals and guests like the Palmers, who waved and said hello, knew to take their walks long before the temperature gauge rose into triple digits.

Something else that occurred in the wee hours of the

morning: a blue-colored note had been stuck to her door. She ripped it off, folded it once, and stuck it into her pocket, hoping she'd remember to read it before too much of the day had gone by. To be honest, she was beginning to get comfortable running the inn, making small tweaks to the operations here and there. Sticky notes notwithstanding, she hadn't yet met Ethan in person, though his voice—and handwriting—were unmistakable.

Willow tugged at the leash, eager to sniff and poke around outside. The minute she'd gotten all of her shots, she seemed to realize the world was her oyster. "C'mon, girl," Melody whispered. "How about you do your thing so I can get back inside for a cup of coffee, hmm?"

They tottered along, Melody yawning and Willow taking her sweet time, when her cellphone's ring startled them both. Have mercy! Melody answered before she'd had a chance to think it through.

"Have you read the paper?"

Melody sighed at her brother's brusque greeting. "Good morning to you, Tom, and, no, I didn't read the paper." She almost added: *I'm not a retired octogenarian* but thought better of it.

"You need to stop that guy, Mel. He's dragging your reputation—*our* reputation—through the mud!"

Melody zeroed in on Willow's bed head as she sniffed and circled, finding the perfect spot to relieve herself. Even this moment was far more enticing than talking about her ex-husband and his latest headline-grabbing shenanigans.

"I haven't spoken to him in months, nor do I plan to."

"Are you serious?"

Melody frowned. Her brother hadn't offered to help her move nor even asked her one question about her new job or living situation. It was Jane, her sister-in-law, who checked to make sure she'd made it safely to Florida in her ten-year-old Honda. She made a mental note to check caller ID next time her phone rang before sunrise.

"Didn't take you for such an early riser."

Pause. Then, "It's new."

Melody shifted. She and her brother weren't particularly close, but they weren't usually at odds either. If she were to try to characterize their relationship, she would have to say ... dependent. Throughout their lives, their relationship was dependent on *her* direction. Getting together for the holidays? Only if she called with an invitation. Need help with their father before his passing? Only when she requested assistance.

One-sided would be another phrase that came to mind. She blew out a breath during the silence. "If you have a problem with Scott, you need to call him directly."

"*I do?* That's *nuts.*"

"Do you need his number?"

"Sis."

"Bro."

This time, the heaviness in his pause was palpable. They had turned a corner and he knew she wouldn't be doing him any favors this time. She continued, "In case you're wondering, I have a new life here in Dragonfly Cove and I don't care to revisit the old one. If that's something you would like to do, then I'm sure Scott will answer your call or meet you for coffee to spread his lies. But I won't be intervening."

"As if! By the way he keeps a big crowd around him, you'd think that coward was running to be president of the United States, and not some lowly town mayor."

Curiosity poked its way into her head. Scott had always been so restless, pushing her to move here and there. The last place they'd landed reminded her a lot of Stars Hollow from the *Gilmore Girls* series. Secretly, she'd hoped they would put some roots down there.

Little did she realize that she would be the one to leave. Scott had found his footing there, his home—he'd made that abundantly clear. Oh, how she would regret this. With a sigh, she asked, "Fine. What is it that's got you so upset?"

The silence from her brother filled her mind with ... worry.

"Tommy?"

"She's pregnant."

A ferocious blast of cold, like ice, overtook her, and Willow took that exact moment to relieve herself a second time.

She couldn't speak. Or react. Instead, she just stared after Willow who stepped away from the puddle and shook off the moment, the jingle of her collar ringing like a morning alarm to the surrounding guest rooms.

If only a simple shake of her head could erase what she had just heard.

"The thing is," her brother continued, no doubt oblivious to the building emotion in her, "he's going on about it, telling anyone who'll listen that you never wanted kids. Even said it on TV."

He didn't! Couldn't! A sear of pain tore through her chest, sending a volley of aches through her core. Questions filled her head, but she had no room for answers. The dreaded sweat that had been finding its way over her skin lately appeared now, even before sunup.

"What are you going to do about it?"

She swallowed and exhaled in an attempt to bring coolness to her limbs. Willow turned back to their studio apartment, and Melody followed behind her, grateful for direction. Quickly, she scooted the pup back inside, then stood in the doorway.

"Sis?"

"Nothing. I'm going to do absolutely nothing."

"But did you hear what I said?"

"I did, and I have to go."

"You have to do something about him, Mel. People talk."

Willow had already curled up in her crate, unbothered by the dark cloud making its way through Melody's heart.

She snapped a look back out the door and westward toward the sea. "I heard you, Tommy."

"And?"

"And ... I'm going to the beach. Goodbye." She disconnected her cellphone, shoved it into the pocket of her hoodie, then stepped quietly back outside.

The problem with walking with one's head down, fully hooded, is that you cannot see where you are headed. Maybe obvious to some. Then again, with such a wide swath of beach, one would think that other beachcombers could avoid a collision with an aimless wanderer who was deep in the weeds of troubling thoughts.

Unless said beachcomber was wandering aimlessly himself.

Their shoulders collided.

"Very sorry. Are you all right ...?"

Melody rubbed her shoulder. There wouldn't be a bruise—it wasn't that hard of a hit—but the jolt had broken off a piece of the crust that had hardened further on her phone call with Tommy.

"I'm fine. Sorry. I wasn't looking where I was going."

"You sure you're okay?" Dark eyes searched hers, a hint of familiarity in them. As a woman alone, she knew she should dart away, but the softness in his gaze—like he was truly concerned that he'd hurt her—made her stay. And that voice …

She straightened, with a hint of realization. "Ethan?"

An awkward pause waited as they stared at one another.

Finally, he said, "You're my new hire."

New hire. Hmm. It had been two months, but okay …

"Can't you sleep, Melody?"

Probably the most personal thing he had asked her since she had arrived in Dragonfly Cove. Her job interview had been conducted by phone and consisted of the usual investigative banter.

What are your qualifications?

Are you able to commit to a move?

How do you handle guests under foot?

And her personal favorite, *Can you make a decent cup of coffee?*

Other than that interview, after she'd shown up for her first day on the job, she and Ethan had not interacted. Well, except for the sticky note diaries. Others might not find such an arrangement workable, but, as an adult with all kinds of ideas, in a way, she relished it.

She nodded. "Early morning phone call."

"That'll do it."

"And you?"

At first, he tilted his head to one side, confusion in his

expression, then a sliver of light dawned in his eyes. "Early riser."

His eyes crinkled at the corners, as if a humorous thought came to mind, but when he didn't share it, she looked away. Had she been staring?

"I've never been one myself, except by default. Hotels don't sleep, so I've had to learn to pull myself out of the warmth of blankets even when I haven't wanted to." Even as the words flew from her mouth, she realized how intimate they sounded. If only she could take them back ...

He opened his mouth as if to respond, but, in a flash, his gaze hardened into a frigid stare. Great. Melody pulled her hoodie more tightly around her.

"You can't be cold," he said.

She narrowed her eyes. She could be whatever she wanted. Cold, hot ... annoyed. She caught herself before responding with the first thoughts that came to mind. No sense ticking off the boss.

Sea water pooled around her feet. "I'd better get back," she said, finally.

He shifted. "My note. Did you see the one I left on your door?"

"I saw it." She hadn't read it, of course, but she wasn't lying.

"Supplies are getting low. You can handle shopping, I presume."

"Supplies ...?"

"For the inn." The wrinkle of his brow told her he thought she wasn't too bright. That annoyed her more.

"Okay, for the inn. Sure. I can do an inventory and fill in what we need. Do I need a purchase order?"

"This isn't the Holiday Inn."

She looked for a crack of a smile, but, when it didn't appear, she shuffled her feet, waiting.

His voice softened. "I'll leave a credit card number for you at the desk."

"On a sticky note?" The words tumbled out of her mouth before she'd thought them through.

This time, his mouth flattened into hard lines, joining the coolness of his gaze. "Just find out what's been done before. Understand?"

"Understood." She hesitated before asking. "Before you go, you mentioned in my interview that you'd like me to be the eyes and ears of the inn."

He shifted again, waiting for her to continue. It was unnerving but she pressed on.

"From my experience, I see areas where we can, um, make check-in a little smoother." She swallowed, thinking back on the software she'd already researched. "And Frank has mentioned that he has time on his hands, so ..."

He still stood there, silent, only this time one of his eyebrows rose in a question.

"So I'd like to give him some projects in the lobby and dining room. Just some touching up and perhaps moving things around to accommodate the influx of guests this summer."

He was still quiet and oh, how she wanted to roll her eyes at his lack of response. Finally, she said, "Do I have your permission to move forward?"

"Within reason."

This time, she was the one who waited for more. When it was obvious that *within reason* was his response, she nodded. "Thank you."

He nodded back, and then continued down the beach. It was about time for Melody to get back to her apartment so she could shower and check on breakfast at the inn, but, if she turned around now, she'd end up walking alongside her gruff-ish boss.

No, thank you.

She lingered a moment, swirling her toes in the briny water. A deep intake of breath allowed the salt air to fill her lungs.

Her new boss was a strange bird, and her job rather uncomplicated, a little dull even, but, despite all that, a sense of gratefulness came over her on the walk back. She needed this job, this new life, far away from the drama she'd left behind.

As Melody stepped inside the studio apartment she now called home, her puppy barreled into her shin and gave her bare skin a few enthusiastic scrapes of tongue. She scooped up the wiggly creature.

"Sweet baby. Did you miss me?" A soft tongue licked her cheek. "I'll take that as a yes."

She put Willow back down and pulled off her hoodie to dump it onto the back of the dining chair. A blue wad tumbled out of her pocket. The sticky note. Melody released a garbly sigh and peeled it open.

The inn needs supplies.

She laughed out loud. No wonder Ethan looked at her like she'd lost her mind. Then again, what kind of boss leaves notes on his employee's door while she's asleep.

The kind whose employee lives within spitting distance of her job, apparently.

Willow yelped. Melody bit her lip and wondered if the neighbors could hear her pup. She scrolled through her phone for Leslie's and hit dial.

"Buongiorno!"

"Buongiorno to you too, Leslie."

"Everything all right with Willow? With you? How are you two getting along?"

Melody smiled. She kissed Willow's pillow soft head. "She's heavenly. I'm exhausted but happy."

"Bellisima!"

"Sounds like you're getting ready for your Italy trip. Would you happen to have time to fit in a coffee break before you leave? Or maybe I should say cappuccino?"

"I'm already here! Italy is everything I had dreamed it could be ..." Her voice turned breathless.

"Oh, wow. You're kidding. I guess, well, I didn't realize you'd be there already."

Leslie laughed, the sound of it like happy little bells. What might that be like to let loose such unfettered laughter?

"It's been weeks already," she said, "but I suppose you have been busy with your little darling and hadn't noticed."

"I guess you're right."

Sound like air whooshed on the line and Leslie's voice turned distant. "Nico? What is it, my love?"

A man's voice responded. She couldn't make out what he said.

"So sorry, Melody," Leslie said when she came back on the line. "We are about to take a Vespa ride through the hills and I will be meeting my boyfriend's family. I cannot wait!"

"I'd better let you go then."

"You had a question, no?"

"Nothing that can't wait. I'll see you when you return to the States."

"If you need advice about your baby, go see my friend, Emily. You'll find her working at Barks & Brews. Pretty. Wears all black. Can't miss her!"

Melody laughed. "Okay, I will."

"Bring your pup—and relax. Order an Aperol Spritz!"

A smile lingered on Melody's face, Leslie's enthusiasm contagious. "Will do. Enjoy your vacation already!"

"I will! I am! Ciao!"

Her boyfriend's family. Wow. Hadn't Leslie just met Nico? She vaguely remembered talk about her meeting a man online and taking a whirlwind trip to Italy to meet him in person. Some might find that dangerous, but Melody thought it ... romantic. She hoped that Leslie had fully vetted the stranger.

Sigh. Despite her own rocky love life, she still believed in happily ever afters. Even a part of her longed to turn back the clock.

She huffed another sigh. All Melody really knew about her boss was that he was a longtime widower with no children who happened to own a "gently loved" inn near the coast. Even that was more than her business to know.

When Leslie showed up with a potted plant and a card with Ethan's name written across the envelope with a flourish, she thought, perhaps, a little flirting was going on between them. The woman was full of chatter about traveling and her beloved dogs, though, and Melody hadn't wanted to pry. But now she knew.

Maybe it was simply a birthday gift. Who knew that Leslie, the well-loved local dog breeder, had her sights already set on a hunky (she assumed) Italian?

"Well, little Willow, I guess it's time we venture out and make some friends of our own at Barks & Brews."

Taking a dog to a bar. Was that really a thing? "It's either that or I'm going to have to figure out how to train you all by myself."

Ever since Leslie mentioned an Aperol Spritz, Melody had craved one. It was late afternoon, the sun still hot and balmy. A perfect day—then what day wasn't in Dragonfly Cove?—for a refreshing drink.

Willow rested in the shade beneath the small round table, a generous bowl of water at her side, her paws still wet from sloshing them around in her drink.

From Melody's vantage point on the vast grounds of Barks & Brews, she could see inside the bar to wood-sheathed walls beneath a peaked roof. Hung on those walls were vibrant paintings from a local artist of azure surf, golden sunshine, and a rainbow of people enjoying it all.

When the waiter delivered her orange aperitivo filled with ice, Melody thought she could hear angels singing.

"That's a generous pour." A woman with dark hair and a white lap dog, its hair shorn, called out to her from two tables down. "Does it taste as heavenly as it looks?"

Melody took an icy cold sip and breathed in the bitter-sweet scent. The day had been long, both her feet and mind were tired. "It is. Like angels conspired to make me the perfect drink after a crazy day."

The woman laughed. "You've convinced me."

Melody gestured to the empty seat across from her. "Feel free to join me. Is your dog friendly?"

The woman waved a hand and stood up, holding her pup in one hand. "Give her a treat and she's yours for life." She took the seat across from Melody. "I'm Lola. This is Henry. And who's this little girl under the table?"

"This is Willow."

"Oh, like a tree!"

"Exactly. I had a favorite one back home that made me happy, so I named her for it."

"I love that."

"Is Henry named after someone special?"

Lola nodded, a sly smile on her lips. "Well, I thought of naming him Thoreau or Wadsworth ..."

Melody laughed. "So Henry it is. You must like poetry."

"I love all kinds of words, truly. I'm an editor." A waitress with long blonde hair in a ponytail stopped by then, and Lola said, "Bring me one of what she's having, will you?"

"Absolutely!"

When the waitress had gone, Lola asked, "Where is back home?"

"I'm a recent transplant from Ohio."

"Ah, welcome. Think you'll miss the winters?"

"Let's see. Chapped fingers, cracked skin, three layers of clothing just to go outside to check the mail ..."

Lola held up a hand. "Got it. Say no more." Her drink was delivered. She took a sip. Her eyes lit up as she held up the glass. "Where in the world have you been all my life?"

Melody laughed. "In Italy—my friend is vacationing there and insisted I come here to have one and take a break with Willow."

"Sounds like a good friend."

"Honestly? I hardly know her. She told me about this place because a friend of hers works here." Melody glanced around. "But I don't see anyone resembling her here."

"That's okay. You can talk to me." Henry peered over his owner's embrace, spotted Willow, and yapped. For her part, Willow stood up on her hind legs, tail like a windshield wiper. In her excitement at meeting Henry, who was still rather suspicious of her, Willow dribbled some pee.

"Sorry about that," Melody said.

Lola gave Willow a pet and spoke in a baby voice. "She's just a happy girl. Aren't you, sweet thing? Yes, you are."

Abruptly, Lola looked up, and her tone changed. "Have you been to the dog park yet?"

"Not yet. I've been keeping Willow away from other dogs until she had her shots. She has them all now, but, honestly, I'm not sure I'm ready."

"Why not?"

Melody shifted. In her life, she had whitewater rafted down the Kern River, and backpacked through Yosemite's wilderness, but one thing she had never done was penned herself inside with who-knew-how-many unknown dogs.

Lola waved a hand. Melody noticed she did that a lot. "It's settled. We'll do it together. My little guy likes to run with the big dogs, so, hopefully, we can stay together and I'll show you the ropes. Oh! And you'd like Hank. He's usually there training dogs and showing off his tats."

"What?"

"You'll know him by his tattoos, ha-ha! So, you'll go with me?"

Melody finished her spritz and shot a look around the beachy, dog-friendly bar. It was getting late, but the weather held up. *You're really not in Ohio anymore.* She looked at Lola and nodded.

"Yes. It's a plan!"

Lola squeezed Henry closer. "You hear that, buddy? I think I found you a girlfriend."

Chapter Three

A week had passed uneventfully since Tommy had ruined her morning with the revelation about Scott's pregnant girlfriend, the woman he had cheated with, and Melody was determined to bury all thoughts of them forever. Unfortunately, ten years' worth of marriage could be difficult to forget. She thought of him during the simplest of actions, such as brushing her teeth in the morning (he always squeezed the toothpaste in the middle) and making coffee (he preferred light roast to her dark).

And yet, her new surroundings at the inn, including the small-town beach vibe and the new faces—especially Willow's—were all helping her create new memories that would, hopefully, one day replace the ones she wanted to forget.

"How in the world have you managed to keep her a secret so long?" Maria patted Willow's head, then dropped her a turkey treat when she sat without prompting.

Melody smiled, quickly snapped a photo of the moment, then shoved the phone back into her pocket, regretting the sting that picture-taking still caused. Another memory that she hoped to erase.

It had been a busy day already with several guests lingering in the dining room and two couples arriving hours before check-in. For the most part, Willow stayed content in her crate beneath the window—a miracle for sure. Well, she stayed put until she heard Maria, aka "dog spoiler," enter the small lobby.

"It's not on purpose—the inn accepts pets, after all. And she's not exactly a secret."

Maria sent her a side-eye.

Melody shook her head. "I just haven't mentioned to the boss that we have a new—"

"Assistant Manager?"

"Something like that." She didn't mention their collision on the beach a week earlier. "Besides, as you know, he's been traveling again."

"Which means fewer sticky notes for you."

"Yes! No sticky notes for me!" She paused. "And does it matter anyway? For all we know, our mysterious inn owner is a dog lover."

Maria laughed heartily.

"What?"

"I'm just not so sure about that. He's always telling you: Do this! Do that! Take out the garbage!" She tsked. "If you ask me, Mr. Cranky-Pants could use a few dogs to bring his spirits up."

"Shh."

"Oh, you know that's something we can agree on!"

Melody laughed. "I'll plead the fifth. Now, I better get this girl outside before the unthinkable happens."

"You mean, your boss shows up with dark chocolate and a promise to be nicer?"

Chuckling at Maria's sense of humor, Melody grabbed a chocolate mint from the counter where it was sitting next to one of Maria's dog-eared romance novels. She popped the chocolate into her mouth. "Hm-mm. Delicious." She shook her head. "You know I was talking about avoiding an accident—a puppy accident. And I can buy my own chocolate, thank-you-very-much."

"Watch it with that attitude! You might never find a husband that way."

Melody's smile froze. With Maria, she had found a partner-in-crime of sorts, but their relationship revolved solely around the management of Sunny Cove Inn and nothing much else, well, unless you counted chatter about raising a puppy.

Maria called herself the chief of sanitation management in that she spent the majority of her time tidying up behind guests sashaying through the main guest house to pour themselves a cup of coffee or a sip of wine. And since she was hired one day later, she addressed Melody simply as "boss."

Outside of work, which admittedly took up most of Melody's life at the moment, the two didn't mingle. As cheerful and warm as Maria was, Melody wasn't sure she wanted that to change, especially now that her ex's face had started to show up on social media due to a viral meme. Something about a baby slapping him on the cheek during a townhall meeting...

Anyway, she kept trying to leave that life behind, but, as the saying goes, the internet is forever.

So was family. Tommy had called her twice since he'd dropped his little bombshell with no warning, but she had let it go to voicemail both times. She still did not want to talk about it—to him or anyone else—so, while at work, she kept that smile as bright as she could. "I'll be back in a flash."

Outside, Melody walked Willow along a finely-combed dirt path that wound its way around and through the inn's property. Though it was late morning, the ground was not yet hot enough to be a concern. Besides the main house, there was a multiunit building in the back and a pool house with plenty of shade for visitors. But Melody's favorite part of the property was the garden that a team of two kept both neat and natural looking—no hedge boxes anywhere. Honestly, it was the one place on the entire property that did not need any sprucing up.

She relaxed on a shaded bench beneath a tree and watched the world stroll by. A woman with silver spikey hair walked swiftly by, a leash in her hand, an obedient bright-blonde pup walking evenly with her. Melody squinted. That pup could be one of Willow's siblings.

"Would you look at that ... a puppy that doesn't pull at all." She turned a look on Willow, her nose inserted into a thicket of beach grass. Melody's phone pinged, so, with a sigh, she took a look at the screen to find a text from Jane, her sis-in-law.

Scott on social media. Baby bump photo shoot with the hussy. Saying he always wanted to be a family man!!

Melody's thumb hovered over the text box. So much she could say right now. So much she should write back, and yet, what would she say at this point?

Didn't her brother and sister-in-law understand how much she wanted to walk away from it all? She had left behind everything she knew and moved more than a thousand miles away to prove that point. So why did they constantly feel the need to send her reminders about the past that she had said goodbye to?

Maybe ... maybe because it affected *them* so much. She imagined that they were hearing it from locals when in the grocery store. Or maybe people were turning away when they strolled by, embarrassed for them.

Revenge wasn't pretty, but, oh, Melody fought off the urge to dish some out to Scott.

With a huff, she turned off her phone's ringer and plunged it back into her pocket. Some might say she'd lost her will to fight. That question pinged in her mind as well, volleying about without a clear place to land.

Whatever the reason for her reticence to confront Scott or post a counterpoint on social media, it wasn't like she was hiding in a corner somewhere, not living her life to the fullest. On the contrary, she had plenty to focus on in her life. More than enough.

Like the pup chewing on a neatly manicured clump of beach grass.

"C'mon, sweet girl. Let's give Lola and Henry a call."

He was skinny and wore a jogging suit that reminded her of a leopard. Or maybe a leopard *costume*. Only she'd never seen one with short sleeves like this one. (Not that she'd ever really seen any leopard jogging suit before.)

With his black, curly hair and bevy of tattoos—even on

his neck—Hank the dog trainer stood out among the otherwise nondescript Floridians milling about the dog park in their beige shorts, tees or tanks.

A woman with a large-brimmed hat attempted to hand over her dog leash to Hank, but the Jack Russell Terrier with jackrabbit tendencies encircled her until she became tied up like a mummy. One wrong move and she very well could end up doing a faceplant into the lawn.

Hank smiled congenially, gently coaxing the animal to "leave it" with a simple halt of his hand. When the pup had calmed, the dog trainer spun the woman around like a top until she was no longer in danger.

Melody smiled at the show. For all her trepidation about coming here to Heritage Park, a happy peacefulness filled her. She had passed Leslie's home on her walk over, giving her even more warm fuzzies as she thought about the first moment she had met her sweet Willow.

Lola came up from behind. "Well, chop chop now, let's go inside." She opened the gate, took off Henry's leash, and put him on the grass. But Henry would have none of it, choosing instead to curl up on top of Lola's pink Cloud slides.

Lola released an exaggerated sigh. "You're making me look bad, kid."

"Let me see if Willow can help. She hasn't played with other dogs yet, well ... other than her siblings. This is all very new." Melody unhooked Willow's leash.

Immediately, Willow bumped Henry with her nose, and he in turn sent her some kind of warning. But it must not have been too scary because Willow hopped away and began to run like a bucking bronco who had been freed from her pen. Henry pursued her like a spurned lover.

Melody and Lola watched from the sidelines, both

laughing until they could barely breathe. Lola whipped out her phone and took a burst of shots. "How are you not taking pictures of this?" Then she waved her hand. "Forget it. I'll send you some of mine."

At one point, Henry and Willow ran a loop around Hank and his student, again and again, until his Jack Russell protégé could no longer ignore the frivolity. The peppy dog broke away from the trainer and catapulted over Henry, his hind end landing on Willow. Best free entertainment anywhere.

Minutes later, Willow appeared at Melody's feet, tongue looser than gum dripping from a hot car. As Melody began to unscrew the top of her water bottle, Lola stopped her.

"Oh, friend, this is a *luxury* dog park. Come with me." Henry trotted after her until they reached a water fountain at his level. Lola pushed a lever with her foot that provided a continuous stream of water for dogs to drink from.

"Willow, would you look at this!"

They both laughed as Willow ducked in and out of the water stream, both drinking and taking a dip in it.

"Guess I'm going to have to give Willow a bath after her bath." Melody pulled her pup gently away from the water so another dog could have access. She shook mightily, spraying water on them both.

"I'm so sorry!" Melody said, hopelessly throwing up her hands in a weak attempt to block the shower of doggy droplets.

"It's all good." Lola ran a hand down her shorts. "Now I won't have to shower later," she quipped.

Melody patted Willow and said, "Go dry off now."

While the pups continued to frolic in their freedom, Lola said, "What would it be like back home right now?"

Melody sighed and leaned back against the fence. "Hot, thick air, full sunshine."

"Like here."

Melody smiled. "Yes and no. There's no ocean there, but the lake is nice. But no salty breeze or long walks along the gulf."

"Enough said." A knowing smile made its way onto Lola's face as she kept her gaze focused in the distance where their dogs were fast becoming best friends. "Bet you left behind a big beautiful house out there, though. Even a bungalow is expensive here."

"Not really. I've never owned a house. My, uh, well, we moved quite a bit, so we rented."

"We?"

A beat passed. "Ex-husband."

"Ah. So you came here to—"

"Start a new adventure." This time Melody didn't skip a beat with her answer, nor did she care to hide from her past.

"Good for you! I've never been married, but I had a boyfriend for a long, long time, and let's just say I like dogs better than men."

"Understood."

Just then, Henry broke away from a pack that had formed and trotted over and lay down at Lola's feet. "See what I mean? Devoted to me."

"Totally devoted!" Melody agreed.

"In all seriousness, Mel—does anyone ever call you Mel?"

"Sometimes. You can if you'd like."

"In all seriousness, Mel, I hope you find what you're looking for. Dragonfly Cove is an *exceptional* place to begin again. My advice to you is to start filling your nest with the things you love—are you thinking of buying a place of your own? Because I know a great real estate agent."

"No. I'm living at the Sunny Cove Inn. No plans to move."

Lola raised an eyebrow. "Sounds like a retirement home."

"It really is a lovely little inn—"

Lola waved a hand. "I know the one. One of my aunts stayed there ages ago. Cute as a button, though a little rundown if you ask me."

"Noted. Some areas could use an update. I'm the onsite manager there. Not a huge salary, but I have a spacious studio to live in and that's fine with me. In fact, I should be getting back soon as I have someone watching the desk for me right now."

"Well, my advice to you is, wherever you lay your head at night, make that place your own. Cozy, extravagant, avant-garde—whatever lights you up!"

Make that place your own ...

Melody liked the sound of that and let herself feel the words as they moved like a digital billboard through her mind.

Lola didn't know it, but Melody was starting to wonder if she truly understood herself well enough to know what "lit her up." She'd always deferred to Scott, for some reason, as if bending to his will and tastes would keep the man content. She was no patsy. But for the longest time, keeping the peace made more sense to her than pushing Scott to do anything or live anywhere that she preferred. All she had really ever wanted was to live in peace with him, wherever that was.

And, in the end, she'd lost him anyway.

Another week dragged by, but Willow's growing body did not appear to be on a slow, dragging timeline. Her trunk stretched long, her limbs thickening and lengthening too, and Melody had quickly learned to buy the fifteen-pound bag of food so she didn't have to schlep over to the pet store as often.

Not only did that save her money in food in the long run, but she was less apt to fill her cart with doggy toys.

With a hand poked into her hip, Melody looked around her apartment and tsked. "What am I gonna do with you, Willow?" She gathered up toys strewn about and plopped them into the doggy playpen, the one that she was quickly outgrowing. She groaned, however, at all the mounds of coarse, white stuffing cluttering the ground. Sadly, Willow's stuffed animal, Mr. Crocodile, had met his swift end under the guise of "play."

"I wonder if Hank the dog trainer could teach you not to kill your toys, Willow."

For her part, Willow sat nearby and watched her quizzically, leaning her head to the side. Melody reacted by placing a gentle hand on her chest. The tugging on her heart was unmistakable. And surprising. Becoming Willow's human mom had opened a locked box of emotions that now seemed to spring from their metal walls with abandon and no notice whatsoever.

"You precious little thing!" She reached for her phone, framing the shot in her mind, but her momentary elation waned. Would she ever find joy again over the simple act of snapping a photo? She shut her eyes, wishing away the seared image, the one that haunted her still. It refused to leave her mind. Maybe someday …

Mercifully, her phone rang, and she answered with little thought to who it was.

"Melody?"

"Good morning, Ethan." She hadn't spoken to him since that morning on the beach, although he had left plenty of sticky notes in the night auditor's handwriting. She laughed inwardly thinking of the poor guy taking middle of the night calls from the boss and writing down his instructions. "How may I help you today?"

Pause. "Some guests will be checking in."

Melody grabbed a pen and notepad and waited.

"We—I have known them for many years. The Randells. They'll want the, uh, breakfast casserole. Tell the chef no turkey meat or low fat, low-calorie anything. They'll want real meat. And cheese."

"The works. Got it." Her pen hovered. "Is there anything else?"

Long pause. She might have thought he had hung up, but she could hear him breathing. Her mind drifted to seeing him on the beach and knowing him by his voice. There was a soothing quality to it, like the constant hum of a lush fountain …

She straightened to shake the thoughts from her brain. Willow found her tail and began to spin, trying to catch it in her mouth.

"How is your shoulder?" he asked, finally.

"My … oh!" Melody let out a light laugh. "Perfectly fine. And you? Are you okay after our, uh, collision?" It was so long ago but seemed right to mention it.

His voice deepened. She barely heard him utter the

word *collision* with a sort of surprise derision in his tone. "Of course. I'm fine."

Of course ... cause you're a big strong man? Sigh. Did she really just let that thought enter her head?

Melody pressed her lips together. She'd never met someone so hot and cold in the same conversation—and she wasn't happy with herself for reacting to it with sarcasm. Before the discovery that her ex was cheating, the act of jumping to conclusions wasn't an integral part of who she was.

Ethan cleared his voice. "That's all I have for you today. Good day now."

Now, see? That was pleasant enough. She really needed to focus more on the positive.

She shook away the picture in her mind of Ethan's dark eyes assessing her on the beach and instead spied the empty space that she had created after hauling away the bric-a-brac that had been there when she'd moved in. Frank in maintenance had assured her that she was free to discard anything she didn't want, and she had. Apparently, the former occupant was a collector of sorts.

An unintended consequence of all the decluttering was the creation of a space that now looked far too hollow. Even Willow's presence and toys had done nothing to truly fill it out well.

She dialed up Frank.

"Yo."

"Just the man I wanted to talk to."

"You tease me."

Melody laughed. "Would you bring the armchair and ottoman that's taking up space in the hall behind the front desk over to my studio?"

"I could do that. You know they don't match exactly. Think there might be a rip in the side of the footstool."

"All the more reason to get them out of the inn."

"Comin' right up."

An hour later, Melody stood back, admiring the way the empty space had taken on a homey air. After Frank had dropped off the pieces, she pulled a nubby, gray throw out of her cabinet and draped it over the chair. She folded a similar, cozy blanket and laid it across the ottoman, covering up a tiny tear. She also took one of the bedside nightstands and relocated it to her new sitting area and topped it with a lamp.

There. All it needed was a cute pillow—she added one to her shopping list—and then her new reading corner would be perfect.

"Pretty sure Ethan will be glad I found a way to recycle this furniture everyone's been tripping over," she said to Willow, as if her pup were human. "Now, if only there was a way to be sure if he'll love you as much as I do once he finds out I'm a plus one now!"

Willow circled and sniffed the chair. She slowed, as if she was just about to ... "Willow!"

Melody quickly scooped up the dog, grabbed the leash from a basket by the door, connected it, then ran outside. Whatever Willow thought she was about to do, she'd lost interest. Apparently being picked up mid-thought could do that to a dog.

As if a squirrel had dropped from a tree, Willow lunged forward with no notice and let loose an unending series of high-pitched barks. A mom in running tights and a tank was looking at her phone while walking alongside a young girl navigating the sidewalk on her Radio Flyer tricycle.

Melody tightened her grip as Willow lurched again, a

squeaky whine piercing the air. The little girl cried, jumped from her trike, and ran to her mother.

"I'm so sorry," Melody called out, hoping the mom would see, like she did, that Willow just wanted to play.

Instead, the woman scowled. She shoved her phone in her pocket, picked up the tricycle, and led the little girl back the way they had come.

Chapter Four

Melody stood beneath a summer moon, one hand wrapped around Willow's leash, the other holding her lightweight robe closed. Beneath it she wore jammie pants and a black cami with fabric so stretched from overuse that it hung to just above her knees.

So attractive.

Willow had just done her business, but that old moon up there kept Melody out for a beat longer. What a difference a few months made. Last year at this time, her eyes were pointed toward the earth, her worries many. She had vacillated between divulging in self-pity (how many pints of gelato were too many in one sitting?) to wanting to book a ticket to a far-off place where she'd never been before. Africa? Tokyo? Spain?

"You're running away. Why don't you stay and fight?" Jane said when she mused aloud at where she might go. And the words still burned. She'd wanted to protest, but something inside of Melody knew that there was a niggle of truth to what her sister-in-law had said.

After her husband's betrayal, and the way she had discovered what he had done, yes, Melody wanted – no had to get far away from him. Surely there was something better out there for her to find, a life that could still shimmer out of the ashes. For whatever reason, despite rejection, she always held out hope for something better.

Soon after that day, she'd called Jane, wanting to prove to her how decisive she could be. "I've decided where I'm going."

"Of course you have."

"I've put in my notice at the hotel and have accepted a job running a quaint old inn on the gulf of Florida.

"You're ... kidding."

Melody remembered pulling the shears away from the window and glancing into the graying sky. "An average of two-hundred-forty days of sunshine on the gulf."

"And you think a little sun is going to fix your heart?"

She paused. "Well, it's a start. And to be honest, yes. Yes, I think the change of scenery will help." She didn't mention she hoped that new faces would assist her in starting over too.

Fast forward to tonight. As Melody stared into the inky sky illuminated by a silvery globe, Willow tugged on her leash and whimpered. "Ready to go in, love?" No answer.

Instead, her growing pup dodged around her, tail thumping. She lunged toward a shadowy figure, and Melody wasn't sure whether to correct her pup's behavior or be thankful for her protective nature.

"What are you doing out here?" The low timbre of the man's voice caused Melody's heart to yelp—with a little extra thumping too.

The man continued. "It's midnight and—"

Willow again lunged at the man, only playfully this time.

Ethan?

Her boss stopped, his mouth open. His eyes shifted and he reached a hand down to let Willow check him out. "Who's ... this?"

Here we go. Melody *had* planned on making introductions soon, but the right time had not presented itself ... until this balmy summer night.

Wonderful.

She was just about to make an excuse about how she meant to tell him about the puppy she adopted, but life had gotten so busy, and—

He was squatting on his haunches now, holding Willow's face in both of his hands. Her puppy, who had an unusual amount of energy at midnight—aka the "zoomies" —held angelically still as her boss fussed over her, his voice unusually high pitched. Almost as if he had put some kind of spell on her.

If only she could borrow some of that super cool energy for those early mornings when Willow leaped on the bed to wake her up whether she wanted to be awakened or not.

He looked up at her, eyes curious. The light caught his salt-and-pepper stubble. "What's her name?"

Melody cleared her throat. "This is Willow."

Ethan put his face perilously close to her pup. Isn't there a rule about not doing that ...? "Willow. Like a tree. I like that." Willow licked his nose, and he laughed. "I'd say she likes the name too."

With noticeable reluctance, Ethan stood and stuck his hands in the pockets of his jeans. "She's young. Maybe three months old?"

"Four. Though she's growing so fast, she seems older."

"Still has the mind of a babe, I'd say."

Melody laughed. "True."

"And the reason you're outside at this ungodly hour is ... training season?"

Melody sighed. "You got it. At least I'm here and not still in Ohio."

Ethan stared at her for a long beat until understanding lighted his eyes. "Right. You're a transplant here."

"Yes, and there's something so different about being near the gulf coast, especially at night. Even the air smells like the sea. I like that. Gives me comfort." She paused. Why was she waxing poetic to the boss?

He nodded. "I'm from the Midwest, too, moved here because of ..." His voice trailed and his eyes focused on the distance before swinging back to hers. "Well, I moved here and never looked back."

Now it was Melody's turn to nod. "I can understand why."

He gave her a small smile, his gaze thoughtful.

Willow, who had been snuffling at Melody's feet, melted into the ground as if turning in for the night. As if on cue, both Ethan and Melody laughed. Their eyes caught, laughter stilling, though a smile remained on both of their faces.

"Guess I'd better get her home."

"I'd say." He stood there, one hand in his pocket. "I'll watch you both get in safely."

Melody tilted her head, looking for some sign that he was teasing. He wasn't.

"'Night now." She began to walk toward her studio, Willow suddenly full of energy again and straining toward Ethan. Melody slowed and called over her shoulder. "Willow says good night too."

He chuckled.

Inside, Melody spotted the cozy nook she had created. Goosebumps alighted on her skin—the good kind.

She had been hoping to get to know Ethan better, to get a feel for how she might improve upon the inn—not just clock in every day—and, she reasoned, breaking down walls between them was a mighty first step.

Maybe, she had *misjudged* him. It was difficult to get to know someone through the limitations of square sticky notes. Maybe Ethan wasn't gruff, just busy and preoccupied. All the more reason for her to not concern him with the updates she might like to make to the inn, both with procedures and some of the basic decor. He'd already given his okay *within reason.*

Something released in Melody as she thought about this while slipping out of her flip flops. She looked down at her summer robe and gasped. Oh, brother ... "Willow, why didn't you warn me I was talking to the boss in my jammies!"

Willow quirked her perfect little head to the side. If eyes could shoot out emojis, hers would release hearts into the air.

Melody brushed her hand across her pup's head, a small laugh slipping out. "It's okay. I forgive you."

She scrunched her eyes, wishing away the picture in her mind of standing outside while chatting with the boss in her less-than-new sleepwear. To Ethan's credit, he made no mention of what she wore. Nor did she catch any kind of judgmental gaze running down the length of her.

Instead, he played with her dog—the animal he knew nothing about—and provided cover until she was safely inside.

Melody rested her hands on her hips, and stood in the lobby of the inn, gazing around with fresh eyes. For the first time since her arrival, she no longer felt like she was simply passing through. Last night's unexpected encounter with Ethan helped significantly. One night under the moon, she in jammies and he smitten with Willow, had softened awkwardness into something more amicable. She'd thought about it all night and this morning.

Newfound strength had appeared, giving her the confidence to take stock of the space in front of her, and all the things that weren't quite right.

Like this lobby. Charming ... but cluttered. A collection of mismatched furniture filled the space—some too large, or worn, and most of it outdated. The floral print couches reminded her of her Aunt Gracie, who she always loved— God rest her soul. But she'd been gone for more than twenty years, and those couches should go too. That and the paint-chipped shelves that held an odd assortment of knick-knacks like the ones she had ousted from her studio.

"They've got to go."

Maria strode up behind her. "Talk to yourself much?"

"More than I'd like to admit." She chuckled. "Just saying out loud what is crystal clear in my head this morning."

"And?"

Melody swept her hand through the air. "All of this has to go. Looks more like someone's cluttered attic in here rather than a welcoming bed-and-breakfast. Don't you think?"

Maria shrugged, then turned toward the desk. "You know what they say," she called over her shoulder. "One man's treasure and all that."

Melody bit her lip. Except for Frank, all the staff was fairly new around here. She had asked him once about Ethan's late wife, Naomi, but all she could pull from Frank was: "She was a nice lady."

By the looks of things, she had been gone a very long time. Yes, the inn was tidy. The paint was fresh. Screens in good shape and no broken doorknobs anywhere. But otherwise, from the little she had gathered, the inn had a revolving door that ushered staff in and out like tourists.

In some ways, it reminded her of life with Scott.

Let's move to the mountains to experience snow.

So she had packed her puffy jacket and moved.

Let's find a lake somewhere and create a love nest there.

So she'd packed a swimsuit and moved.

I need city life. Let's get away from all this dreadful quiet.

Each time, Melody had requested a transfer to one of their sister hotels, packed a pencil skirt and comfortable heels, and followed Scott to the next "perfect" place for them to settle.

As she looked around the lobby of the inn, envisioning the changes she wanted to make, warmth filled her—and not from a hot flash either. Her "nest" might be small, but, for the first time in a long while, Melody felt more at home here than she had anywhere she had landed with Scott.

Now to address the "things" that appeared to have stayed behind even as staff came and went.

"Less is more, right, Willow?" Melody murmured as her puppy dozed beside the desk, her large paws twitching as if chasing a dream. "Time to declutter and refresh."

She walked around the space, mentally cataloging what she wanted to change. The old, round rug in the entry, with its faded pattern, would need to go eventually. She envisioned something simpler, maybe a coastal blue or soft cream that would make the lobby feel airier. The heavy curtains blocking out the sunlight? Definitely out. She'd replace them with sheer, breezy drapes to let the Florida sun flood the room.

The phone rang, pulling her from her thoughts. Maria had disappeared so she jogged over to the desk. "Sunny Cove Inn, this is Melody," she said, keeping her voice bright.

"Hey, boss!" It was Chef, calling from his small office off the kitchen. "On the other line with the supplier. We're low on a few things, so I'm placing an order. Anything else you want to add?"

Melody glanced at her notebook, where she had already started making lists of ideas for the inn. "Did you see the list I left? The items Ethan requested for his guests?"

"Yep."

"Great." She thought a moment. "Since you've got our supplier on the phone, could you add some fresh linens— lighter colors, maybe white or something neutral?"

"You got it."

She hung up to find Maria standing next to her. "I just gave the cleaned rooms the white glove treatment. All ready."

"Excellent!"

"So I was thinking. I'm planning to stop to look at barstools for my husband, Rick, tonight. Anything you want me to price for the inn while I'm there?"

Melody grinned. "Sure. See if they have any deals on accent chairs."

"For the lobby?"

"Mm-hmm. Not sure if we have the budget for it, but might as well see what's out there, right?"

Maria laughed. "I've seen you eyeing this room with your hand on your hip more than once!"

"You have not."

"Right. You've been itching to do that since you got here. I'll get on that on my way home!"

After Maria disappeared down the hall, Melody reviewed the incoming guest list, double checked that all notes had been reviewed, and that there were plenty of fresh baked cookies waiting for those soon-to-arrive—a new procedure she started with the chef just last week. He had made chocolate-macadamia, very tropical and her favorite.

She was lost in thought when the front door swung open. The familiar clatter of the bell brought her back to the present, and she looked up to see Lola saunter in with Henry in tow. "Hey, friend. Working hard or hardly working?" Lola joked as Henry made a beeline for Willow.

"Lola!" Melody stepped around the desk to give her friend a hug. "I'm plotting a little makeover for the inn, and I have you to thank."

Lola raised an eyebrow, her eyes lighting up. "Now that sounds like fun, but why me?"

"You inspired me to feather my nest, which I did with my studio. But since I spend the majority of my time over here—"

"You extended the feathering!"

Melody pointed. "Exactly."

Lola pressed her lips together and gave the place a thorough sweep of her eyes. "I always thought this place could use a facelift," she said. "Need help?"

"I wouldn't say no," Melody replied, laughing. "It's

mostly small changes for now, but I think it'll make a difference."

"I can't wait to see what you do with the place. You've got good taste," Lola said, as Henry and Willow began their playful dance, darting around the lobby. "But how's our little troublemaker? Have you been practicing the training?"

Melody groaned and threw up her hands. "Not even close. Willow's such a sweetheart but imposing. Little children are afraid of her, and I'm in way over my head. I've tried watching videos online, but they make it look so much easier than it is!"

Lola nodded in agreement.

"I was thinking of asking Hank for help."

"Hank's a good call." Lola looked lovingly at her dog who was currently rocking forward and back, egging Willow on. "He worked wonders with Henry. I'll text him and let him know you're interested."

As Lola grabbed her phone from her purse, Melody looked out the window, her mind drifting back to Ethan. She wondered if her ideas for the inn were *within reason*, but didn't want to disrupt her forward momentum. There was still a part of her that feared his reaction, mainly because he wasn't the easiest person to read. Was there an invisible line she should not cross?

"I can see those wheels turning," Lola said, looking up from her phone. "What's up?"

Melody sighed. "It's Ethan. He's been ... better, lately. Friendlier, even. But I don't know what he'll think about some of the ideas I'm proposing. The inn was his wife's before she passed. No one seems to know much about that, except Frank. And he's pretty quiet."

Lola softened, leaning against the check-in desk. "I get it. You don't want to push too hard, but, at the same time, you've got good ideas, and this place needs your touch. He'll come around."

"I hope so."

Lola put a hand on her shoulder. "You'll figure it out. I believe in you. And if not? You'll stick around until something better opens up that better uses all that creative talent in your head."

The door creaked open again, and in walked Hank as if answering a summons. His usual laid-back demeanor was intact, though, like a wrangler with a leash coiled in his hand, he seemed ready to get to work.

"Did I hear someone needs a little puppy training?" Hank asked, flashing his easy grin.

"Such service!" Melody laughed. "I think 'a lot of puppy training' is more like it."

Hank crouched down to pet Willow, who bumped her nose against his hand. "Hey there, girl." Didn't take long for Willow to flop onto her back and offer her middle for a good belly rub. Maybe Maria's words about her pup being teachable would prove true.

"Good luck with the training there, Hank," Lola said, a tad sarcastically.

Hank smirked at Willow, "We gonna let her call you out like that, my girl? Nope. No can do." He stood up. "How about we start with some basic commands? You'll be a fast learner. I know it."

Willow turned up her chin and howled.

Maria reappeared in the lobby, a question in her eyes. Melody said, "Maria, I'd like you to meet Hank—"

Hank walked toward her and reached out his hand. "Friendly neighborhood dog trainer."

"Makes house calls too," Lola cut in.

"I can see that," Maria said before turning to Melody.

"Want me to work the desk so you can take a break to teach sit-stay-paw?"

"Bless you! That would be wonderful."

Together they all walked down the street, past Leslie's house, and through the gated entry of the neighborhood dog park. As Hank began working with Willow, guiding her through sit, stay, and leave it, Melody couldn't help but smile.

Willow was a fast learner, and, with Hank's guidance, maybe they would be able to curb some of the more chaotic tendencies—like lunging at little children on tricycles! As she watched the training session unfold, and peace came over her, her mind wandered back to the inn.

She could feel change coming. Excitement trilled through her at the prospect of unleashing a bit of creativity in the life-worn inn. It was the same hope she'd felt when she'd made the decision to leave behind her ex and his drama and embrace a new life in sunny Florida.

Yes. She'd transitioned from poking along in the dark to feeling empowered and on the cusp of something new. She couldn't wait to see what happened next.

Chapter Five

Willow and Henry chased each other on the lawn outside the bar as Melody sat at a corner table watching the spectacle. The air spun with light and warmth, chatter and clinking glasses ... and the occasional, playful bark. This was the third time she'd stopped by and considered making it a routine to end her evenings here whenever possible, especially after meeting up with Lola and the dog park crew.

Ah, Dragonfly Cove, you've bewitched me body and soul. She smiled at the comparison to the Mr. Darcy line that popped into her head as she reflected on the easygoing town with dog-friendly charm that was quickly becoming home.

If only she could bottle up this feeling and douse herself with it whenever trepidation and fear crept in, two emotions she was working hard to keep at bay, especially when receiving text updates from Jane with tidbits about Scott's campaign—and growing family.

Lola plopped down beside her, breathless from corralling Henry. "I swear, that dog has the energy of a toddler!" She took a long sip of water before giving Melody the once over. "You doing okay?"

Melody nodded as Willow wandered over, tongue hanging out. Her dog took a long drink from the water bowl under the table and then curled up for a snooze. She didn't care to talk about her ex, and instead gave her friend a rather vanilla response. "I'm getting there. Between Willow and work, I've had my hands full but I'm relaxing into the moment. Truly, I am."

Lola raised an eyebrow. "Speaking of work, how's everything at the inn? Any more changes?"

"Slowly, but surely," Melody replied, stirring her chai latte, which had started to separate. "I've switched out the linens in the dining area. Nothing too drastic, but it's already making a difference. Guests have been complimenting the fresh look."

"Good for you! And Ethan? He okay with it?"

Melody hesitated. "He's an elusive guy, so I don't really know. But he gave me a budget early on, and I've been able to stay within it. I am a little nervous for him to find out that I've stopped using three-by-five-cards in a recipe box to keep guest information on."

"Ha! I think that's charming."

Melody wrinkled her nose. "I found software that's very simple and has a free trial. Slowly, I'm building our guest list in it. Just hope he sees the benefit of using tech for data."

"Wow. Well, you are making progress." Lola said with a wink. "I love that you have a vision, that you're not someone who just clocks in without any care to making things better."

Melody nodded but felt a twinge of uncertainty. Had pushing forward with her ideas hurt her marriage? She'd read once that first borns should never marry each other, mainly because their birth order made them stubborn and unyielding (among other amazing traits, of course). She always thought it funny because both she and Scott were first-born children in their respective families and seemed to be doing well.

Until they weren't.

The last thing she wanted to do was push forward with ideas and cross some sort of line that took her right out of the job that made this move possible.

"Your server's on break so I'm stepping in. Can I get you ladies anything else?" Her nametag said Emily.

"You're—I think we have someone in *common!*"

Emily gave Melody a confused smile. "Do we?" She glanced under the table and gasped, then immediately squatted to give Willow some pets. "Oh my goodness! Is this one of Leslie's?"

"Yes, ma'am."

"Hi there, beautiful." Emily stroked Willow's soft coat. "You're my Daisy's sister ... did you know that, hmm?"

"How is your pup doing?" Melody asked.

"Ha. It's definitely not boring with her around. But she's adorable. I often have her with me, but not today." She gave Willow a couple more pets. "You're more golden than my girl, sweetie, but, otherwise, you look so much alike!"

Emily stood, smiling.

"I think we're good with drinks, but I have to ask before you go—how's Leslie? She's the one who recommended I come here."

"And told her to order the Aperol Spritz!" Lola chimed in.

"That sounds like Leslie." Emily's brows knitted. "To be honest, I'm worried about her. Thought she'd be back by now ..."

"Oh?"

Emily shifted her stance, concern still etched on her face. "Did she sound okay when you spoke with her?"

"Honestly, yes. She sounded happy. She was using Italian words and getting ready to go on a Vespa ride, if I recall."

Emily raised a brow. "With Nico?"

Melody thought for a second. "Yes, I believe that's what she said. Something about meeting his family."

"Okay. Yes, she told me that too but I haven't heard much from her." Emily shrugged and let out a small laugh. "I guess I worry too much. She met that guy online and, well—"

"You're just being a good friend," Melody said.

Emily hung her head. "I'm mothering her."

"That's exactly what good friends do," Lola added.

A flash of sound split the din of the restaurant. Emily rolled a look upward and smiled. "Ah, they've fixed the streaming service. I was missing the music in here, weren't you?"

"I did think the barks were louder than usual," Melody said, instrumental music filling the place. "Hadn't realize it was the absence of music."

"I know my blood pressure has suddenly dropped," Lola quipped.

"So nice officially meeting you ladies." Emily glanced down at Willow and Henry. "And you two cuties. Hope to see you all again soon."

When she'd gone, Lola tilted her head to one side, scrutinizing Melody. "Your wheels are turning."

Melody coughed out a laugh. "What in the world does that mean?"

"It's almost like I can see a thought bubble forming over your head."

Melody leaned forward and offered up a little shrug. "I was just thinking that a little music might do the inn some good. Not sure why I hadn't thought of it before."

"Sure it would. A little Zeppelin or Motley Crue, perhaps?"

Melody scrunched her nose. "Was thinking jazz."

"At least make it the Latin kind—not that elevator stuff."

"Maybe some Sinatra, Martin, or Davis Jr. ..."

"How old are you? Ninety-two?"

"They're classics! But maybe you're right. I should focus on contemporary crooners like Michael Buble and Harry Connick Jr."

Lola rolled her eyes. "Yeah, sure, whatever."

"The idea is to welcome our guests with light and calming music, you know, sort of set the tone for a relaxing weekend."

"Snort."

Melody smacked the table, awakening both dogs. "Stop that."

Her friend's eyes popped open as if she were waking up, and she glanced around asking, "Where am I again?"

Melody shook her head, cracking up. "Fine. I'll rethink the playlist, but I still like the idea of adding some mood music to the place. I'll give it some thought."

A whistle caught both women's attention. Both women swiveled to find a hulk of a guy standing beside an equally impressive-looking dog, a German Shepherd. Emily approached him, and, though the two weren't touching, they were leaning in, both animated.

"Oh, wow ..." Lola said, still watching.

"Yeah." Melody couldn't look away either. "He kind of reminds me of Bradley Cooper."

"With extra ripples."

Both women laughed, then lifted up their glasses, and clinked them together with a hearty, "Cheers!"

The lemony sun cast a soft glow through the inn's lobby windows. Melody had awakened early, taking Willow for a jaunt before the ground became too hot for her paws. Now, she wandered into the inn, letting the night auditor go home. After a quick check in the dining area, ensuring breakfast preparations were underway, she stepped behind the front desk and scanned the incoming guest list.

Last night, she'd lounged in bed with Willow snoring by her side, working on a soft but engaging playlist. *Nothing too boring,* she'd thought. The music was meant to set the tone for guests as they came down for breakfast, milled about, or checked in, weary from their travels.

Melody poked her gaze through the open doorway to the dining area, spotting the perfect tabletop for her travel speaker. She plugged it in and opened the app on her phone, her fingers dancing over the screen to control the playlist.

Success!

"Music to my ears!" Maria bustled into the lobby with a stack of fresh towels in her arms.

"Nice, right?"

"Sure beats the kitchen clatter. Where'd you find the speaker?"

"It's mine. I was hoping to find one here, but the only

thing in that old closet is covered in dust and looks like it belongs in a museum."

Maria laughed. "I avoid that closet. It's a time capsule from the 80s."

Mr. Ross, from Room 4, appeared at the foot of the stairs. "Good morning, ladies. Is there coffee for this old man?"

Melody chuckled. "You're not old, sir."

"Maybe I'll believe that after my first cup."

Maria led him into the dining room with a grin. "Right this way, sir."

As more guests trickled in, the music drifted softly through the air, blending with the hum of morning activity. Willow stretched in her crate beneath the table, her paws twitching as she dreamed. No doubt she'd be on "clean up" duty after the morning rush had gone, but, for now, dreamland.

Melody watched as guests exchanged sleepy smiles, her mind drifting between the calming music and the small improvements she had made.

A little plant here, fresh linens there, and now music, she thought. Small touches, but they breathed life into the inn. Her eyes fell on the dull beige drapes. She still wanted to replace those, but wouldn't Ethan prefer to be involved?

She bit her lip. He had told her some changes were fine

...

Before she could dwell on it, a wave of unease crept up her spine. No matter how much she focused on the inn, whenever she stopped moving, her thoughts increasingly returned to him—Scott.

She tried to run, but even a thousand miles away wasn't far enough to hide. He was still out there, parading his new life, his new girlfriend, and their soon-to-be baby in front of the cameras. His mayoral campaign had somehow become a stage for their personal history, and he wasn't shy about using it.

Melody clenched her jaw, recalling the latest article that Tommy had forwarded to her. Scott had casually mentioned how his *first wife* had "never been interested in children." He'd said it with a smile, playing the victim, as if he hadn't been the one who shut down every conversation about starting a family. And when they'd finally tried—she had tried so hard, had wanted it so much—he abandoned her the moment it became clear that their time had passed.

Melody rubbed her temples, her thoughts swirling. Moving to Florida had been her salvation. She'd left behind Scott and the lies that had littered the path to their divorce. But no matter how far she ran, the sting of his betrayal still reached her.

Willow stirred and slipped out of her crate, awarding Melody with a giant, downward dog stretch. She smiled despite herself. This little pup of hers had become a bright spot, a reminder that starting over was as close as one decision. She couldn't bear to think of all the love she would be missing if she hadn't followed Leslie's advice to adopt her girl.

"Melody?"

Startled, she looked up. Maria had returned, this time with a steaming cup of coffee and placed it in front of her. "Everything okay with you today?"

Melody forced a smile. "Just thinking."

Maria slid into the chair across from her. "I know you don't talk about this much, but I have to confess: I saw the memes about your ex making a to-do in your old home town," she said softly. "Scott."

Melody's stomach tightened. She didn't want to talk

about it, but the concern in Maria's eyes was clear. "I'm sorry. I know you don't want to hear it so I won't repeat what was said," Maria continued, "but if you ever need to vent, I'm here."

Melody stared into her coffee cup, the steam curling like past ghosts. "He's twisted everything," she murmured. "Like *I* was the problem. That I didn't want kids." Her voice faltered, and she took a shaky breath. "But I did. I wanted a family so, so much."

She hated the way her voice broke but continued. "And when it didn't happen... he just gave up. On us. On me."

Maria reached across the desk, squeezing her hand. "You don't owe anyone an explanation, Melody. The people who matter know the truth."

Melody nodded, but uncertainty gnawed at her. She hadn't spoken to anyone about it other than Tommy and Jane. She and Scott really hadn't lived in that town that long, so her friendship circle was pretty small. They'd all been part of couples, anyway.

She glanced down at Willow, who was watching her with big, trusting eyes. Melody scratched behind her pup's ears. "Willow, my love, you're the best decision I've made in a long time." She lifted her gaze to Maria, her voice lightening. "So good to have this sweet creature who couldn't care one whit about my past."

Maria smiled. "She's a sweetheart. But neither do I or any of your new friends here. I promise you."

Melody looked toward the window, where that sugary morning light was growing brighter. She suddenly felt the urge to get outside, to feel the ocean breeze and clear her head. "You're so kind." She walked over to the basket and plucked out Willow's leash. "Now that things are getting quieter, would you mind keeping an eye on the desk? I'd like to take her to the beach."

Maria nodded. "Good idea." On Melody's way out, Maria said, "And don't let that jerk ruin your day, okay?"

"I promise."

With Willow bouncing beside her, Melody stepped out into the late morning air. The ocean breeze kissed her skin. Something about it made the weight of the past lift.

As they walked briskly toward the beach, she realized something else: She had no control over Scott. Not when they were together and certainly not now.

She could ask him to stop with the theatrics and the drama he'd made up. She could even threaten to tell the town the truth—that he'd cheated and that the woman carrying his child did too.

She could even divulge the cruel way she had discovered their secret.

Yet she had made a decision once, and she only needed to remind herself again what it was: to move on. She had not realized when she'd made that decision that she would be faced with veering away from it every time something mean or petty or untrue was posted online.

Whatever indecision she faced, one thing remained: She could not control the past, but she *could* continue to guide her thoughts toward the life she was building here in this small town on the gulf of Florida, where she had swapped out willow trees for lengthy, swaying palms.

If she stayed the course, kept her eyes wide open, the hope inside her told her she could find the peace that she'd always wanted. As the salt air hit her senses anew, this truth seeped into her core.

As Willow tugged toward the shoreline, and Melody followed, she smiled. Today, she'd focus on the little things

—the music in the lobby, the sand beneath her feet. Little changes that made all the difference.

Tomorrow? She would have to be brave enough to ignore the boulders sent her way in favor of larger and better changes to come.

Melody hadn't seen Ethan in two weeks. No sticky notes left on the computer, nothing stuck to her door—just a single email asking her to remind housekeeping to sweep the doorframes for cobwebs. He never shared his schedule with her, but she wondered if he had been traveling.

As if showing up to personally answer her musings, Ethan entered the lobby in the late afternoon, just as a couple paused to compliment her on their stay and to give Willow a treat from the bowl on the counter—another one of Melody's additions to this pet-friendly inn.

Willow took the treat to her crate. Melody smiled and thanked them, but her focus was on her boss. His eyes swept the room with a practiced gaze, and then, without a word, he ducked his head around the corner where she had placed the small travel speaker.

For a moment, he seemed to freeze in place.

Melody stepped toward him, explanation on her lips. "I thought a little music would help set the mood. Do you like the selection?"

Ethan's expression remained still, but something flickered in his eyes—a shadow she had seen before but could not quite figure out. His gaze drifted to the speaker, then back to her eyes.

"The guests seem to like it." Why did she do that? Fill in the silence like that?

His lips tightened, and quietly he said something she couldn't make out.

"I'm sorry. I didn't catch that."

"Turn it off," he said quietly.

Melody blinked, caught off guard. "I ... I thought it was a nice touch. It's background music."

"Turn it off," Ethan repeated, more forcefully this time, though his voice wavered. Willow sauntered up to him and sniffed his sneakers.

Melody hesitated, unsure what to make of the sudden tension in the room. His gaze dropped to the floor for a brief second before lifting again. "Please."

His tone wasn't harsh but pleading and layered with something deep and fragile. Willow must have noticed it too because she stayed blissfully calm. Melody may not have ever lost a spouse in the same way, but, instinctively, she too connected with Ethan's pain.

Without another word, Melody reached for her phone and opened up the app that controlled the playlist. The music stopped, leaving a heavy silence in the room.

Ethan gave her a stiff nod and turned on his heel—walking toward the office—then suddenly stopped. He looked down at his heel to where Willow dutifully shadowed him. She almost thought he might shove her away or tell Melody to put her back in the crate.

Instead, he bent down and gave her ten seconds of head rubbing. Then he stood and walked briskly toward the back office.

Had his shoulders always slouched like that?

Melody stood with her hand still on her phone. Ethan had been an enigma to her, someone who seemed to know what he wanted, but then suddenly didn't. He was cold and his notes terse yet he could drop to the ground in the middle of the night—and even during the day—to pet her sweet Lab pup.

As she watched him disappear into the office without another sound, Melody began to wonder if she would ever learn to figure him out.

Later that afternoon, Melody found herself alone in the dining area, absentmindedly rearranging table settings for the next morning. She couldn't shake the look in Ethan's eyes from earlier, the way he'd reacted to the song that had been playing in the background—if that even was the source of his pain. She still didn't know.

"'Afternoon, Mel." Frank shuffled in holding a toolbox and wearing a friendly grin. "Came here to fix that loose curtain rod you mentioned."

"Wonderful. Thank you, Frank."

Frank laid a drop cloth beneath the window and set his toolbox on it. Then he unfolded a step ladder. The man was neat as a pin when he worked, something she dearly appreciated.

Frank paused. "Haven't seen this speaker here before. Is it new?" He picked up the single, travel speaker.

"Not new, but I poached it from my studio to try it out in here."

"Hmm. Music, huh?" He scratched his chin thoughtfully before continuing his work.

"Yes, I put on some soft jazz in the lobby earlier."

"Makes sense."

"I thought it provided ambiance. Of course, if we make it a regular occurrence, I suppose we'll have to subscribe to a service."

Frank frowned.

"If you play music in a business, you're supposed to pay a subscription fee, so the artist gets compensated."

"Never knew this."

Melody shrugged. "Just a random fact I picked up from years in the hotel industry."

Frank climbed up the two rungs of the ladder, holding a drill. "Then I'd say that's not random at all."

"Maybe not."

With the quick zip-zip-zip of the drill, Melody went back to work preparing for check-in. She was assigning rooms to incoming guest dockets when Frank showed up at the desk. "Finished already? Wow—you're so fast I hardly noticed.

"That's my job. Get in and out and don't disturb the guests."

Melody smiled.

"Is that speaker giving you trouble? Need me to tinker with it?"

"That? Oh, no. It doesn't look like much—no long wires or seventies-style knobs—but the sound quality is fantastic."

Frank let out a low hum. "You found that old stereo in the closet, didn't ya?"

"I did. And, to be honest, it reminded me of something from another decade. I've lived through quite a few of them." Melody laughed.

He chuckled dryly, shaking his head. "I remember when those were brand new at the five-and-dime—that's like today's Walmart."

"I knew that."

"You're too young to know that."

"Thank you, Frank. You just made my day!"

"I'm old enough to remember playing records on my father's hi-fi so I'd look cool in front of the ladies."

"You're teasing! You're not that old."

"Now look who's making someone's day." Frank's grizzled face split into a grin. "You know, I tried to get rid of that dusty old stereo once. It's broken and useless, but the boss won't let me touch it."

Melody frowned. "Why wouldn't he want to get rid of an old stereo that doesn't work?"

Frank paused again, his expression thoughtful. He scratched his chin then swung his gaze to hers. "I don't think it has anything to do with the stereo unit, but who it belonged to."

"Naomi."

"Yes. She loved music." Frank's voice turned quiet. "Classical stuff, mostly. She used to play it every day in the lobby, right in that spot where you put your speaker. After she passed, I think Ethan couldn't bear to hear it. As far as I know that old stereo's been gathering dust ever since."

The unmistakable sense of dread that precipitates a hot flash spread through Melody. She was beginning to recognize the triggers, in this case, stress. She glanced toward the corner of the dining area where music had been flowing from that little speaker into the lobby just a couple of hours earlier.

"I didn't know." Melody bit her lower lip. "Ethan never talks about her. He didn't mention that she once played music in here."

"He wouldn't," Frank replied, his tone matter of fact. "He doesn't talk about her much. As an old-timer, I'm the only one who's been here long enough to know that some things are harder to let go of than others."

Melody swallowed hard, her limbs turning cold from the layer of sweat on her skin. She hadn't meant to stir up painful memories, but it was clear now that she had.

"I didn't mean to ... hadn't meant to ..." She looked at Frank. "He came in here earlier and asked me to turn off the music. He's so hard to read, but, honestly, I should have made the connection."

Frank gave her a reassuring but sad smile. "You didn't mean any harm. He knows that. But you gotta understand, the inn is more than just a business to him. It's tied to her memory in ways most people wouldn't understand."

Melody nodded slowly, her mind racing. When she had interviewed for this position, she'd had the feeling that Ethan was not all that interested in running the inn. She even commented to a friend after she hung up that her new boss seemed more like an investor than an innkeeper.

But then he'd started leaving her all those notes, many of them instructions on what she deemed trivial matters. Melody had been drawn to the inn because of her romanticized ideal of starting over in a quaint place where she could leave her own imprint.

She had not realized how tightly the Sunny Cove Inn, after all this time, was still bound to Ethan's past, to Naomi. How had she not realized this?

Melody cleared her throat. "May I ask when she passed?"

Frank thought a moment. She expected he was counting the years in his mind. "Almost exactly a year ago."

Melody gasped. She reached behind her for the desk chair. She needed to sit down. "Only a year ago? No wonder he reacted the way he did ..."

Frank offered a small, kind smile. "How were you to know if nobody told you?"

She glanced at the black-and-white framed photo of the woman with the heart-shaped face on the wall behind the desk. Her eyes held both wisdom and questions. She wished they had met.

Frank pushed away from the desk and dipped his chin, as if doffing an invisible hat. "He'll come around, Melody. You're doing good things here. Just give him time."

Melody smiled weakly in return, though the weight of her mistake still made her stomach ache. "Thank you, Frank —especially for sharing all that with me."

He nodded, then strolled back out the door carrying his toolbox, drop cloth, and ladder, and leaving her in the quiet lobby alone with her thoughts.

Chapter Six

As the evening light faded, Melody stood in the now-silent lobby, her hand resting on Willow's leash. Chip, the night clerk, had been running late, so Melody stayed until he arrived. Willow recognized that Chip was here for the night shift and that meant it was time to go home. She looked up at Melody, tail thumping against the hardwood floor.

Melody's heart again swelled with love for the first dog she had ever adopted. "Come on, girl," she whispered. "Let's get you outside in that fresh night air."

Outside, a salt-laden breeze washed over her, and Melody reveled in it, breathing in deeply. Willow's nose wiggled in the air, no doubt also intrigued by seafaring scents flowing from the West.

"That big ocean is brimming with bouillabaisse for you, sweet Willow!" She laughed at the casual way she was beginning to chat with her pup.

Willow trotted beside her, just as Hank had taught her to do, ears bouncing. It occurred to Melody that until

Willow came into her life she had felt very, very alone. Even when married.

But now as she picked up the pace toward the water, she couldn't help but think about how joyful a naughty pup had made her. Despite the heavy thoughts that had tried to derail her lately, Melody laughed aloud.

Impulsively, she grabbed her phone from her pocket and squatted eye-to-eye with sweet Willow. "Sit," she said. "Now, stay put."

Willow did a loop-de-loop and Melody groaned. "I meant. Stay." This time she added both a hand motion *and* confidence in her command—and Willow kept her butt down on the ground.

Melody backed up, still reminding Willow to stay. Her pup's mouth opened, revealing a pink tongue and, quickly, Melody took the shot. Then another. She leaned to the side, knowing she was likely pushing her luck, and took one more picture with her phone camera.

Willow lunged forward and licked Melody on the cheek causing her to roll backward onto the ground. She laughed despite how ridiculous she must have looked. "You silly pup!" This made Willow buck around her like a horse. "Okay, okay, I get it—you want to play. Let's go!"

And off they went, jogging toward the beach, no doubt making a spectacle, her with a giddy smile on her face, and Willow with that taffy tongue blowing behind her like an erstwhile necktie.

This time, the sweat that alighted on her skin was the natural kind, not the soul-sucking kind brought on by life's stresses. As she slipped out of her shoes and began stumping through sand, Melody's mind drifted back to the inn. She thought about the music that played in the background and

Ethan's response ... and Naomi, who she knew only by her photo.

Again, she thought of the grief she knew, of the loss of dreams following the demise of a marriage and rejection by someone she loved, and, of course, over the loss of her parents. But she still could not fathom the kind of grief that Ethan was obviously still reeling from.

The realization that Melody had unknowingly stepped into something so personal in Ethan's life weighed heavily on her. How could she continue to make changes at the inn without dredging up painful memories for him?

Willow tugged on her leash, and, oh how Melody longed to unhook her pup and let her run free. Unfortunately, she had no idea if she'd ever return—she'd have to talk to Hank about that! Instead, she did her best to keep up with the frisky dog who seemed to have more energy as she grew.

As they jogged together along the shoreline, a cool breeze skimming off the water, worry lessened and hope grew. Melody longed to slow just long enough to take snapshots of Willow from the side as she galloped along the water's edge. Then maybe take a few shots from above, like a steady drone.

As she moved along, laughter escaping her, saltwater landing on her exposed skin, an idea started to take root. Maybe music wasn't the only way to breathe new life into the inn.

Her heart fluttered as she thought of her old camera gathering dust on the shelf back in her studio. The last time she had lifted the viewfinder to her eye, she'd been so happy, so excited to capture images of the staff Christmas party. They'd spent months planning something special and memorable—Langley, her boss at the hotel, had even dressed as Santa and given out bonus checks as a surprise.

Exhale. Where might she be now if she hadn't looked closely at that *one* image, if she had not unwittingly recorded what was going on right before her eyes between Scott and one of her coworkers?

She must have slowed her pace because Willow threw a look over her shoulder and pulled on the leash. "Sorry, sweets. Caught me thinking."

The truth is, none of that mattered now because she was right where she needed to be. She smiled in spite of the past. Willow had single handedly—okay, maybe single paw-edly—reignited her love for capturing moments like this one beneath a moonlit sky. She didn't want it to end.

She wasn't going to give up on bringing ambiance into the inn, but she didn't need to rush it. Perhaps she could simply find some art—or a photo or two—to breathe some fresh life into the place.

Tomorrow, she thought, a small smile tugging at her lips. *Tomorrow, I'll see what we can do about those empty walls ...*

Two days had passed since the "incident" and, though she had tried to maintain a routine that put the awkwardness out of her mind, Ethan's expression lingered like a cloud overhead.

"So he just told you to turn off the music? Just like that?" Lola picked up her glass and took a sip of her frothy iced mocha. "Pretty cheeky of him."

Melody and Lola met at Beachside Brews for an afternoon caffeine pick-me-up, and, in Melody's case, a break from the inn that would get Willow outside too. After spending much of the day inside the air-conditioned inn, she'd forgotten that the temp outside was rising.

Melody reached down to pat Willow's head where she lay beneath the table, making sure she wasn't overheating. "It's my fault, really."

"How is it ever your fault?"

She blew out a breath. "Frank—he's the inn's handyman —told me afterward that the previous proprietor, Naomi, passed away only a year ago." She cupped her iced green tea with her hands. "I had no idea. Should have done my homework."

Like most of the new staff at the inn, Melody had believed their boss's grief was long buried. Now, knowing how raw it was, how deep his mourning must still be, she couldn't easily shake off the heavy weight of it, though she was trying.

"If it was going to impact your daily life at the inn, then Ethan should have told you what was off limits. Sheesh." Henry growled softly from beneath the table. A quick *shush* from Lola put a stop to it.

"Enough about me," Melody said, fanning herself. "How's the edit going?"

Lola scrunched her eyes closed. "Honestly, my brain hurts. Too many words trying to fit in there."

"Or trying to get out of there."

"Ooh, ba-da-bump. I see what you did there."

"Edit, as in to strike." Melody laughed, but Lola just shook her head and glared.

"I'm seriously thinking of changing careers. I wonder how much boat crews make?"

Melody's sharp laughter spiked the otherwise quiet ambiance of the coffee shop with bright blue walls. The wooden columns, painted white, made it feel as if they were visiting on a neighbor's front porch, rather than at a coffee house.

"Hey, I'm serious!"

"Oh, so you're seriously going to wear sneakers and a collared shirt and clean up vomit and fish guts?"

"Now, you make it sound so less glamorous than I pictured in my head. Not nice."

"I'm here to help, my friend." Melody took a sip of her tea, hiding her laughter.

Their server, Jasmine, appeared next to their table holding a pitcher of ice water. "Thought I'd give your girls some fresh water. It's a hot one today!" She bent down and added water to the large bowl under the table, which Willow took as permission to take a bath.

Melody gasped but grabbed her phone and snapped a photo anyway. Jasmine squealed a laugh and moved to the next table.

"That's one way to get the shot," Lola said.

"Willow," Melody said, pulling the water away from her, "stop that."

Lola tsked while laughing. "Getting back to your predicament ..."

"Must we?"

Lola looked directly at her, a sobering look on her face. "You can't hide from your boss's inconsistent behavior forever. I know, I know you say it isn't a huge deal, but ..."

"But?"

"It kinda is."

Melody knew she was right. The inn was lovely and provided her a nice home during this transition in her life. But at what cost? She looked up to find Lola leveling a look on her.

"What?"

"You need a hobby, a bonafide interest to help you mentally separate from thinking about the inn all the time."

"Um, I do, and her name is Willow."

"She can help you, but you need more. You need ..." Lola was tapping her chin and looking off into the distance. She swung a look back and pointed directly at Melody. "Photography!"

Melody rolled her eyes. "Been there, done that. I used to take pictures all the time." She didn't mention why she had stopped.

"Well, now you have the perfect model to showcase. Listen, I've peeked over your shoulder at some of those shots of Willow and they're so good, Mel." Lola picked up her phone and wiggled it in the air. "Mine are always such garbage that I thought you had a better phone or something, but you don't. You just have an amazing eye."

For once, Melody didn't protest. She'd felt the same niggling the other night on her walk with Willow, that draw to start dabbling in photography again, only this time, with a subject that wouldn't break her heart. She had even started looking for art to grace the walls at the inn—of course, any photos she took would be for her alone.

"I might just do that," Melody said, glancing at Willow. "If a little someone will cooperate."

"You hear that, puppy eyes? You're gonna get your picture taken." At Lola's tone of voice, Willow jumped up, sloshed her front paws in the water dish before knocking it over, then plopped them both, sopping wet, onto Lola's lap.

Though she knew she should scold Willow properly, Melody just laughed and laughed and laughed.

It was early morning, and Melody stood by the window of her studio, gazing down at the garden, bathed in the golden light of dawn. At moments like this, when the air outside was still and guests still slumbered, the inn felt magical.

Five months. That's how long she'd been in Dragonfly Cove. She could hardly remember the days before Willow, and Lola's friendship—along with the inn staff's—made it seem as if she had been in town much longer.

Willow played beside her, tossing a ball up with her nose and catching it with her paws. Before having a dog of her own, she didn't know just how smart they could be. When she was bored as a child, her mother would tell her to make her own fun. Melody had often protested that.

But as Willow flicked the ball behind her, then gave up chasing it in favor of grabbing her tail and spinning in a circle, she began to think that animals were far more creative beings than they were given credit.

Melody picked up the ball and rolled it along the length of the room. "Here you go, sweetie girl." She laughed as her pup ran to it then jumped on top of it as if she had found the prize all by herself.

Melody's gaze caught on the camera sitting on the small table near her bed and her smile stilled, though it did not break. The other night, she had pulled the camera from its case and left it there to stare back at her, calling her to pick it up again. That Canon camera had been her companion for twenty years, and, in a strange sort of way, Melody felt as if she had blamed her for something that wasn't her fault.

Melody scoffed. *If my father could hear me now, talking about his camera like "she" was human ...*

Still, she had to admit she was happy to see her old friend again. Willow's comical ways had awakened something in Melody—something she hadn't felt in years. Maybe Lola was right, that it was time to let that creative spark grow.

Maria was on duty at the front desk today and promised to holler if she needed anything. So, after feeding Willow and grabbing a quick breakfast of yogurt and blueberries, Melody sucked in a breath, righted her shoulders, and placed the strap of her father's camera over her neck. He'd used that strap to hold his old film camera. When he'd purchased the Canon, she stopped him from tossing it away.

"What are you going to do with this old thing?" he'd said to her, holding up the weathered leather strap. "Wouldn't you prefer to buy something new?"

She reached for it then, giving him a smile. "A new one wouldn't remind me of you, now, would it?"

The big lug nearly teared up at that. Melody released a sigh at the memory, and looked toward the day in front of her. This morning would be the perfect one to capture Willow through her lens.

"Alright, girl," Melody said, crouching down to give her pup a quick scratch behind the ears once they'd made it down the exterior steps to the garden. "You ready to help me with some pictures today?"

Willow's tail resembled a propeller, whirring as if ready to take off. Melody had chosen the long leash today, to give Willow the ability to wander farther away. She looped the handle around a water spigot to give herself two free hands.

Willow investigated minuscule creatures crawling along the earth. Melody also took her time to observe the things she often missed: the rapid wings of a hummingbird zeroing in on its nectar, the way the sunlight dappled wide, flat leaves, and delicate purple flowers blooming along the stone pathway leading to her favorite wooden bench.

She lifted the camera's viewfinder to her eye, framed and snapped a shot. Then another. Then once again she allowed the joy of familiarity to wash over her.

Oh, how she had missed this—the quiet focus of composing a shot, the satisfaction of freezing a moment in time.

It was different now, though. Before, photography had been tied to memories of her past life—her ex-husband, the hurt of betrayal. Slowly, but surely, the memories were being replaced by something new. A small piece of herself was coming back to life, as if the broken parts were healing.

As she moved through the garden, lost in her creative flow, footsteps came up behind her. Probably a guest experiencing the garden too. She turned to say hello but stopped mid-word.

Ethan stood behind her, one hand in his front pocket, watching her, his face unreadable as always. And yet ... a softness underscored his expression today, fewer lines appeared around his eyes and mouth and across his forehead.

"Morning." Melody kept her voice neutral. She hadn't seen much of Ethan since the music incident, and, frankly, she'd been relieved to avoid another confrontation.

"Good morning, Melody." Ethan's gaze scanned the garden, then landed on the camera in her hands before his eyes lifted to focus on hers. "You're taking pictures?"

Melody nodded.

Ethan nodded back, his gaze shifting to Willow, whose puppy brain must've just realized the boss had arrived because she pulled herself away from the succulent her nose had been buried in and galloped toward him.

Ethan cracked a smile and bent down as Willow barreled into him. "How are you this morning," he asked, giving her puppy a few generous strokes. A curl of his hair dipped below his forehead, and, on impulse, Melody snapped the shot.

Ethan froze, one of his brows raised. "Did you just take my photo?"

She swallowed, not sure what to say. Rolled-up sleeves revealed hair on his arms made golden by the morning sun. There was a ruggedness to him that she hadn't noticed before, and a hot flash began to betray her with its rumble over her skin.

"I, uh, yes. One of you and Willow. But if you want me to delete it—"

He smiled, revealing a grin that took ten years off his age. "No need. I just hope you got my good side."

Was that a wink he gave her? She smiled back at him, relaxing some.

"I thought it might be nice to capture some of Willow, maybe even of the inn's charm this way." She held up her camera. "If anything comes out okay, we could put it up in the lobby for some, um, color."

Ethan didn't respond right away. Then, "You look comfortable behind that camera."

"Thanks," she said, her voice soft. "It was my father's."

His eyes held hers for a beat. "I was going to say that I hadn't seen one like it. I suppose that's the reason why."

As quiet settled over them and Willow went back to her snuffling around in the garden, Melody turned back to her camera. She snapped a couple of shots of the way sunlight created shadows across the fountain in the center of the garden.

Finally, Ethan turned to her and broke the silence. "You said something about the walls?"

Melody lowered the camera but didn't look his way. "I was thinking maybe I could put up some of the photos I've taken—just small touches here and there. May even pick up some local art, if you're good with that." She hesitated for a moment before adding, "I won't do anything drastic. Just a few shots of the garden or the beach—"

"Or the owner petting your dog."

She slid a glance at him but couldn't tell whether he was cracking a joke or making a pointed observation. She gave him a casual shrug. "I think it could work."

Ethan's brow dipped slightly, but he didn't look displeased. If anything, he seemed to be considering her idea. Finally, he nodded, though the motion was slow and deliberate as if he was still processing it.

"Why not," he said. "But let me see them first. I'd like to make sure they fit."

There. Right there his reticence showed up again. It may have had something to do with grief, sure. But it also occurred to her that Ethan might be a long, slow thinker, as opposed to Melody's doer mentality. After all, it hadn't taken more than a week for her to plot her exit from Ohio once the truth came to light about her husband.

Still, Melody hadn't expected Ethan to agree so easily, especially after their recent confrontation. But there it was —his tentative approval. She smiled a small but genuine one. "Of course. I'll show you what I come up with before I do anything."

Ethan walked over and stroked Willow's head. "You two have a good morning." He left Melody standing in the garden with her camera in hand and a newfound sense of possibility blooming inside her. Maybe things between them weren't as broken as she'd feared. Maybe, just maybe, they were both starting to trust each other.

After he'd left, Willow bounded over, her leash tangled up and her tail wagging. She nudged Melody's ankle with her nose, so she bent down and scratched behind her pup's ears. "You heard that, huh? I think we're making progress."

Willow barked in response, her tongue lolling out in that familiar, goofy way that always made Melody laugh.

"Okay, my sweet baby," Melody said, "Let's go take some glamour shots of you, hmm?"

Chapter Seven

Melody couldn't believe her luck. She'd found a frame at the drugstore similar to the one that Naomi's photo hung in. She snapped it up. Though she wasn't a fan of the gold edging, she put aside her personal aesthetic in favor of honoring the former proprietor of the inn by hanging the photo of Willow and Ethan in a matching frame right next to it.

"That looks nice there," Maria said, breezing through the lobby with an armful of linens. "He looks happy in that photo. I'm surprised you got him to pose for it."

She left the lobby before Melody could admit she had snapped the photo without giving Ethan a chance to protest. His face was half-turned away, his hand buried in Willow's fur, but the moment had captured Melody's attention and—if she was being honest—her heart too. Willow's exuberance juxtaposed with Ethan's guarded expression drew her attention back to the image ... again and again.

Her gaze slid to the other photo on the wall. Next to Ethan and Willow's hung the small, black-and-white portrait of Naomi that she'd admired every day since arriving in Dragonfly Cove. Placing them side by side told a story, though she'd be remiss to think she could fill in any of the details.

Still, Melody had always loved telling stories with her photos—one reason she'd become a mainstay at events at the last hotel where she had worked. She never wanted to step on the toes of professional photographers who had been hired for weddings, bar mitzvahs, etc., so she had kept her presence understated by capturing candid shots of men in suits, their ties loosened, throwing their heads back in laughter or women leaning in for juicy tidbits heard in a clandestine corner of the ballroom.

Though she might never know many details of the former inn owner—not unless Ethan decided to open up about her—these two photos attempted to tell one of past and present, of lives touched by this inn, and of how life had changed—and was changing still.

She bit her lip as she glanced over at Willow, sprawled out in a patch of sunlight beneath a window, her tail thumping lazily as she dozed. Hank had been texting Melody, urging her not to slow down in training Willow, but the inn had been so busy lately. Guests were filtering in and out, many of them staying longer than they had originally planned, thanks to the unseasonably mild late summer they were having.

Sometimes it was a challenge to juggle room assignments, especially since she and Willow were taking up one of them. A tinge of guilt slid over her then she dismissed it. The small apartment came with the job as part of her pay and willingness to be on call in the middle of the night.

As for the inn, the new check-in system she'd implemented was going smoothly thanks to the simplicity of the software and the staff's ability to learn it. Ethan, for his part, seemed sort of *meh* about the whole idea, but, at the same time, fine with it too. His attitude told her he didn't care much about that part as long as he wasn't the one who had to learn the process and teach everyone to use it.

His hands-off process about this latest change was a win in her book.

Still, she had caught him watching her more often lately, his gaze like a magnet at times, even when guests were milling about. The tension was unmistakable, and she wasn't sure whether it made her glad that he showed some interest and didn't protest her changes or nervous that he was watching her closely in hope that he could pounce if she messed up.

Maria swept into the lobby, one of her flyaway bangs standing straight up. "Such a day already!" She flopped into a chair.

"Take a load off, my friend. You've been moving all morning!"

"Another full house tonight," she said, a fake grumble on her face.

As if on cue, the front door opened and a woman with flaming-Cheetos-colored hair stepped inside wearing an emerald-green romper and white strappy sandals.

"What a charming inn!" she said, approaching the desk.

"Thank you very much." Melody smiled. This was her favorite part of working in hospitality—greeting travelers. "Will you be checking in today?"

"Yes. I'm Maddy Garcia." She handed Melody her credit card. "My husband, Ernesto, is parking the car."

The Garcias would be staying in their largest suite,

which was very private and situated at the back end of the property. "Thank you and welcome to Sunny Cove Inn."

Maddy spun a look around the lobby as Melody completed the check-in process. A handsome man with dark hair, tan shorts and a button-down, and leather slides joined her inside.

"I love the photos on the wall. Are these local shots?" She didn't wait for an answer but turned toward her husband. "Ernie, I can't wait to go to this beach. Oh, and look at the cute dog!"

Speaking of the devil, Willow took that moment to emerge from her crate. She stretched, doing a little downward dog with her behind up in the air, then lazily wandered over to give the inn's guests a couple of hearty sniffs.

"Guess we pass muster," Ernesto quipped.

Maria popped up from where she had been catching her breath. "May I show you to your suite?"

Melody smiled, thrilled at Maria's assistance. Those little touches went a long way toward guest satisfaction. She handed the keys to Maria, who gestured to the Garcias and said, "Right this way."

Ten minutes later, she flounced back into the lobby full of energy. "They're a fun couple," she said. "Asked all about where to eat, what to do. Even gave me a tip!"

"Makes you appreciate where we live, doesn't it?"

"Ya got that right." She took in the beach photos on the wall. There were still many blank spots, but at least Melody had begun to fill them in. "Mrs. Garcia sure loved these pictures. She showed me her Porsche red bikini and told me she was going to put it on and get down to the beach stat!"

"You're kidding."

"No. I almost thought she was about to pull off her top

and start changing right then and there, so I practically ran away." Maria picked up the stack of soiled breakfast linens from the hidden box behind the desk and turned toward the back of the house.

"Ha-ha. I would have liked to see that." Melody paused, throwing a look over her shoulder. "You running away—not the guest in a bikini."

She could hear Maria's laughter all the way through the kitchen.

"Shall I shut my eyes or something?"

Melody's heart jumped inside her chest. She whirled around. "Ethan! You scared me. I-I didn't hear you come in."

The small smile on his face grew.

"Wait," she said. "What did you mean, shut your eyes?"

"I heard something about someone in a bikini ..."

"Ha! Oh that." She waved a hand, though a small giggle rose up. She stuffed it back down.

Ethan stepped closer to the desk now, his gaze brushing over her face. A warmth enveloped Melody, but, for once, she didn't wish to turn down the thermostat.

"I've got something for you." His smooth tone melted through her. "It's not a bikini ..."

She coughed a loud laugh, and a wide grin broke across Ethan's face. He held something by a hanger and pulled off the outer wrapping. "It's a size small. Hope that works for you."

Melody froze. He was holding a pink fleece jacket by a hanger, in her size, with a white logo on the shoulder that read "Sunny Cove Inn."

Her mind ran through several scenarios: the inn had an overstock of these somewhere, someone had returned it, it was a prototype for something they'd thought about selling somewhere …

He frowned. "I've insulted you."

"N-no. Not at all. I … I love it. What a pretty color. But —" she tilted her head to the side while also reaching out to run her fingers down the soft fabric. "I wasn't aware we sold merch."

His smile was questioning, and his brows dipped. "Merch?"

"Merchandise." She cast a look toward the far, rather sparse corner of the lobby. "What a nice idea, but where will we put it …"

"I don't think you understand."

Their eyes caught. Ethan's gaze was unwavering, and her knees decided at that very moment to ask to sit down. Understanding flooded her, though she wouldn't yet admit it. "No?" she said, her voice cracking.

"Melody," he said, "I had it made for you."

She stared back at him.

He cleared his throat. "So you can wear it outside when you take Willow for those nighttime walks."

She swallowed back certain emotions, then licked her lips. "What-what a sweet gesture, Ethan." She remembered back when she had grown cold during their "collision" on the beach. Her mind stalled. There was also the time she stood outside talking to him at midnight, blissfully forgetful that she only wore a thin robe over a warn-out cami.

Maybe the poor guy was trying to keep the guests from ever having to come across that same sight in the middle of the night.

He stepped backward, as if her silence was disapproval. "Perhaps this isn't something you would—"

She lunged for it. "It looks perfect. May I?"

He handed her the hanger, which she quickly ditched onto the desk. She slipped into the comfy fleece and pulled it around her. Maybe a little warm for this time of year, but not at night around the time she usually took Willow out for her final stop for the night.

She didn't want to gush, to make this gift into something it obviously wasn't meant to be. It was simply a giving boss recognizing her need for something better than tattered bedclothes to care for her puppy (and to handle late-night guest emergencies).

Melody nodded, running her hand down the fabric after zipping it up. It could not have been a better fit if she'd had it made to order.

She looked up at Ethan, whose tentative smile reminded her of a teenager.

"It's perfect," she said. "Thank you ... for thinking of me."

Lola leaned across the table, eyes sparkling. "I'm telling you, Mel, you *have* to do this."

Melody smiled but gave her head a quick shake. "Everybody thinks their pup is the most photogenic." Her fingers gripped her glass tighter. Lola had her ear, but Ethan's gesture still held a piece of her heart.

No man had ever bought her a fleece jacket with a personalized logo on it. Was she being silly? She would be a walking advertisement for the inn, after all. Maybe it was just advertising. Advertising in the middle of the night ...

"But your dog really is! And it's more than that. You have this cool instinct that comes through in the photos."

Henry was sitting in Lola's lap at Barks & Brews, tapped out from fifteen minutes of play with Willow and another dog named Leonard.

"Where is all this coming from?" Melody asked, pulling her mind to the present. "What's gotten into you all of a sudden?"

"It's not all of a sudden—did you see the art walk displaying local artwork on the way over here?"

"Yes! I wanted to stop, but Willow was being a pill." On cue, Willow popped up and put both paws on Melody's lap, begging for attention. Melody complied with baby talk and a vigorous massage of Willow's head. "Yes, you are a thorn in my backside, yes, you are, sweet girl."

Lola snorted. "Some of the art I saw was okay, but your photos were a thousand times better!"

Melody tilted her head to the side, giving Lola a dubious look.

"Okay, okay—but at least ten times better. You have to admit that."

"I don't know. Yes, I love the photos I've taken of Willow. They've really helped me personally to pick up the camera again. But"—a small laugh escaped her—"are they truly gallery material? I'm not seeing it."

"Oh, please." Lola rolled her eyes dramatically, tossing a length of hair over her shoulder. "Now, see, that's the problem with you—you refuse to see your own potential. Luckily you have me on your side."

Her friend meant well, and the compliments were a welcome balm amidst the storms, but if she were being honest, her proclamation also stung a little. Melody always felt that she had potential, and she often moved forward with a semblance of confidence.

But there was some truth to what Lola said: When roadblocks were thrown up in front of her, her confidence crumbled until it eroded into a pile of rubble.

Melody had seen this often in her marriage. She had always believed in the idea of chivalry, that her husband would always put their needs as a couple first. She'd trusted him, and he'd abused that trust.

Part of her felt foolish for trusting him in the first place.

"Nonsense," Lola was saying. "You have an eye for capturing moments, and you know it. I've seen it with my own eyes, friend, and, let me just say, I'm jealous. Your photos are special—just like you. Trust me when I tell you, people will love them." Her hand sliced through the air. "Especially pup pics—I mean, look around!"

A part of her knew that Lola was right. Barks & Brews would be the perfect place to display her photos, if they were good enough. Her heart swelled at the idea, even though doubt followed her around like a stubborn shadow.

She scrolled through her phone, viewing several of her recent shots of Willow. Even though she wasn't using a "real" camera, the lighting was en pointe and Willow's energy burst through each frame.

But putting her work on display for the whole town to see?

"I mean, I'm not even a professional," Melody murmured, her voice wavering slightly. "It's just ... something I do for fun."

"That's why." Lola pointed one long manicured nail at her.

"That's why *what?*"

"Do it for fun. Do it because you love it. It's about putting yourself out there—"

"Like I'm on the next episode of *The Bachelorette?*"

"Ha ha ha! They do say that a lot, don't they."

Melody gave her voice a breezy, valley-girl tone. "I'm just putting myself out there, you know?"

Lola cracked up. "That's funny. Hey, maybe you can be on one of those shows for real. I mean, maybe on *The Golden Bachelor*."

"I'm not *that* old yet!"

"Yes, I know, but a golden bachelor would snap you up in a heartbeat."

"Oh my gosh! Stop!" Melody's hands flew to her mouth, laughter overflowing."

"In all seriousness, Mel, you're good enough." Lola still had a smile on her face. "I would love to see your photos grace these walls." Her hands brushed the air.

Within Melody, a hopeful lift sparked. Every day, it seemed, she was given another sign that this move to Florida wasn't some whim, wasn't her running away, but instead her new friends and experiences were all helping her piece herself back together.

Maybe she really was ready to pursue something more.

Before she could overthink it, Lola grinned and waved toward the bar. "Hold on, someone has something to tell you."

Melody raised a brow, watching as Lola waved Emily over to their table. The young woman wore her Barks & Brews apron and a smile with that certain warmth Melody noticed the first time they'd met.

Emily approached with another woman who she'd seen tending bar many times.

"Melody, this is Andrea. She curates the gallery wall," Lola said, her words flowing quickly. "Andrea, this is the talented photographer I was telling you about."

Andrea extended a hand, her smile genuine. "It's great to meet you, Melody. We're getting ready to release these paintings"—she gestured to the striking art on the walls—"to the artist. We haven't displayed photos in a very, very long time and I think yours would be perfect."

Melody blinked, stunned. "Oh, wow. Thank you. I—I'm honored you'd think of me."

"I've always been a sucker for good dog photos," Andrea said, winking toward Emily who laughed in response. "Those shots of Willow are fantastic—almost like she's human."

"Or hoo-man, as we like to say," Lola quipped.

Andrea continued. "We love featuring local artists, and your work has that personal touch we're always looking for. We're happy to put up place cards with your information, so people can contact you—or, if they show an interest, get their information for you."

For the first time, Melody felt a flicker of excitement beneath her burgeoning doubt. Maybe this wasn't as farfetched as it seemed, but ... was she truly ready for this challenge?

"What do you think?" Andrea's eyes twinkled. "Would you be interested in displaying your work on our walls?"

Wow. How long had she tried and tried to get her old hotel to display her work, to see her as something other than the place's front desk operations manager? Melody hesitated but looked to Lola to find her friend nodding her support. A flood of gratefulness came over her, and she found herself nodding too. "I'd love that. Yes. Thank you."

Lola squealed with delight, clapping her hands. "Yes! I knew you'd do it!"

Melody choked up at her friend's unabashed excitement for her. Oh, to return that favor someday ... to offer someone else unconditional joy at their own possibilities!

As Melody sat there, surrounded by laughter, the

sounds of dogs barking, and the scent of coffee beans in the air, a spark of something else snapped in the air for the first time in a very long while: hope.

Melody moved through the inn's lobby, making small adjustments here and there while chatting with Mr. and Mrs. Berardi as they lingered over a cup of coffee.

She had spent the past few days swinging a hammer—much to Frank's chagrin—and hanging framed photos on the wall. She also put up two blue-green seascapes she had purchased at the art festival on her walk home the other day and picked up a couple of pillar candles and holders to add to the lobby.

She didn't believe she was imagining the buzz around the new additions. Guests seemed to linger in the lobby a bit longer than they used to, many admiring photos of the garden of seagrasses, the dappling of light on the beach, and, of course, Willow's face, which looked deceptively angelic, if she did say herself.

One guest, Ms. Bangs from Ireland, had even asked to buy a print of what Melody called Sunset over Dragonfly Cove. "It captures the peacefulness of the town," she said.

After some thought, Melody had politely declined, unsure if she was ready to sell her work. The request had stuck with her ever since, though, her mind rolling a thought over and over. *Is there something about my work that others see but I cannot?*

Just a week earlier, Barks & Brews had called to confirm they would be hanging some of the photos she'd taken of Willow and other dogs on the interior walls. "The boss really loves them, Mel," Andrea said. "She also mentioned that, if you have any of the inn, feel free to drop those off as well."

Exciting news as that was, Melody broke into a sweat every time she thought about her work being up on walls for others to admire—and critique. Well, at anywhere other than the inn.

After the Berardis finished their second cup of coffee and headed out to the beach, the room fell quiet. Hank had come by earlier to pick up Willow for some playtime with other students, and, though she knew a big open dog run was a far better place for her sweet girl, she missed her. Even one of the guests, Mr. Matthews, looked downcast after he peeked into her crate only to find it empty.

Melody hummed as she pulled a shipping box from behind the desk and unpacked a large glass hurricane candle holder. "Ah, so beautiful!" She wiped it down with a soft cloth and let her gaze drift from the table under the window to the coffee table by the loveseat, and back again.

"Guess I'll be getting a bill for that."

Melody sucked in a breath and looked up sharply at Ethan, unaware until that moment that he had entered the room. How did he learn to be so stealthy upon entry?

When their eyes caught, he laughed. "Gotcha."

Melody exhaled. She let out a small laugh. Ever since he'd brought her the pink coat, the wall between them had lowered. In fact, he had not left her one sticky note since then. She should have been happy about that, but, oddly, she still found herself checking the desk each morning for a sign of a note from Ethan.

One thing Ethan had not curtailed, nor acknowledged, was the way he watched her from a distance. She was on to him, having noticed it several times recently—in the kitchen, from the stairway, even when she grabbed a broom to give the back porch a quick sweep. Was he simply watching to see what other changes she was making to his inn? Why didn't he just come out and ask for her plan so they could discuss it?

She held up the glass. "Good morning. You like?"

He leaned against the archway, one hand in his pocket, his expression unreadable. He did that a lot.

"Morning," he replied, his voice low. "I don't have an opinion on the glass."

She laughed.

One of his brows rose.

"No opinion is better than a poor one," she said.

He nodded, a flicker of a smile on his face. His gaze swung to the photos on the walls. There were still plenty of bare spots, something she aimed to change with the right artwork. He pushed off the doorway and stepped over to the desk and stopped, his eyes catching on the photo of Willow and him.

For a moment, the room went quiet. Silence stretched between them, the feel of it both comfortable and charged with something she couldn't name. She studied his face from the side as he looked at the photos on display, the one of Naomi and the other of him with Willow.

Her pulse quickened, tension tightening her insides. Had she overstepped? Did he understand that she was trying to honor them both? Had displaying his image with Naomi's been a step too far?

Mrs. Hess, a guest, stepped into the room, breaking the quiet with a gush of praise. "I love what you've done with this lobby! My goodness, I was here years ago. It was lovely then, but all the artwork and photos you've added, well, you've kept the warmth while raising the ambience. I'm so impressed!"

"Thank you very much," Melody said. "Is there anything I can help you with this morning."

"Yes! I just stopped by for one of those discount coupons you mentioned at check in, the one for Beachside Brews? Thought my husband and I would check out a couple of your bikes and ride over for afternoon coffee"— she leaned in and winked—"or maybe something a little stronger, if you know what I mean."

"Oh, I know all right." Melody nodded and slid a coupon to Mrs. Hess. "Here you go. Live it up, my friend."

Mrs. Hess smiled and looked up toward the sky while pressing the discount to her chest. "That's exactly what we plan to do!"

When she'd gone, silence once again fell like a tarp over the room. Finally, Ethan broke the quiet. "The guests like you." He looked away, toward the far wall again. "And the photos."

"They seem to." Something about the way he said the rather banal words made them sound personal rather than like compliments delivered by a boss. Melody swallowed back nerves that bubbled to the surface.

She made herself step away from the desk and go back to figuring out where to assemble and place the hurricane candle. She had plans to fill the glass with shells from the beach—when she found time for some beachcombing. Maybe if she kept doing what she set out to do, Ethan would go on his merry way, and she hers.

"Well, you've brought something new to the place," he said, breaking her attempt at concentration.

New as in good? She felt so too, though she hadn't

always been sure how he'd feel about the changes. Hopeful-ness unexpectedly bloomed in her chest.

She tried to push away just how his attempts at compli-ments had a buoying effect on her. Not in a greedy way, but the positive reactions made her want to keep moving forward both personally and professionally.

"Yes, they really do seem to enjoy them. I-I just wanted the lobby to"—she chose her words carefully— "reflect some of what I've found so wonderful about living here ..."

"Like Willow."

This time she smiled broadly. "She's so precious that why wouldn't I want to share her with our guests?"

Ethan nodded, his gaze still focused on the photos. "Of course you would."

"Well ..." Her thoughts became frenetic. Why was he here? What was he doing just hanging around and being both suspicious and vaguely humorous?

She swallowed and kept fussing around with the candle, keeping her tone light. "I just wanted to add a little more personality. The inn has so much character already, I-I, well it just needed a little ... refreshing."

Ethan's blue eyes locked with hers. Had she noticed their color before? That they had an unusual gray-blue quality? The air between them shifted—or was she imag-ining it?

"You've made it your own," he said simply.

Melody's throat went dry. Had she really? Did that bother him? How should she respond?

Before she could figure out exactly what to say in response to Ethan's surprise comment, he pushed off the wall and stepped toward the inn's entrance. "I just stopped in to see how things were going, and it appears you have it all under control."

Still speechless, she only nodded.

He turned back before leaving, that lock of hair falling onto his forehead, his voice calm. It sounded less detached than usual. "If you need anything, let me know."

"Th-thank you."

Melody watched as Ethan disappeared through the front door and down the wooden steps, sunlight illuminating golden strands in his otherwise salt-and-pepper hair as he strode along the path and out of sight.

Chapter Eight

Two weeks later, Melody wandered over to Barks & Brews, casting her gaze out to the wide-open field where pups could run amok while their parents relaxed over some refreshments.

It's showtime, she thought, knowing her photography now hung on the walls. She'd been asked to come over after closing one night to help with placement, so, after all the inn's guests had been tucked in for the night—metaphorically speaking—and the night auditor had arrived, she and Willow headed over. The unique venue had looked so peaceful without customers and their pets milling about.

A neat and clean stack of doggy dishes sat in the open doorway of the storage closet, and chairs were stacked on tables. For her part, Willow ran from table to table, gladly scarfing up any leftover tidbits that had escaped the broom.

"Thanks for your help, Willow," Andrea had quipped.

"She aims to please," Melody had said with a laugh. Melody was there to help Andrea choose where the photos would go—not hang them herself. She'd wanted to tell a story in the way that guests would most naturally view them, so she left behind faint pencil markings and notations of what photo to put where.

Since then, the inn had been overwhelmingly busy, so Melody had not had a chance to actually see her photos in their new home.

Or maybe she had been avoiding going over there. Quite possible ...

She inhaled and slowly let it out. *Let's do this.* Upon entering, low chatter, occasional laughter and clinking glasses welcomed her. Beside her, Willow trotted, ears perked, tail wagging. Melody smiled at the way her pup had made this place her second home.

"There's our girls!" Ted, a grizzled, sixty-something regular said. He leaned down from his barstool to ruffle Willow's head. "Ready for your treat, little lady?"

Willow's butt hit the floor.

Good job, Hank. And good girl, Mel, she thought. Though she'd been swamped at work, she had managed to practice *sit, stay, paw* so much that the poor dog was probably dreaming about it like dance students dream about their instruction. *1-2-3 ... 1-2-3 ... sit, stay, paw ...*

Willow's nose twitched, clearly anticipating the biscuit that Ted was fishing out of a small bag on the counter next to his beer. He made her take it out of his hand, then patted her head with a hearty, "Good dog. Now run along."

Willow didn't have to be told twice. She took off running to the farthest corner of the yard, that biscuit held protectively in her jaw.

Ted gave Melody a jagged tooth smile. "They grow up so fast."

She burst out laughing at that and gave Ted a fist bump while moving through the place, waving at other patrons while simultaneously trying not to gasp at the sheer number of photos on the walls in varying sizes.

Andrea swooped in. "So ... the boss made some changes, though we kept your storyline. Sorry to have wasted your time the other night, but do you like?"

Her mind and heart spun, and the smile that pulled on her mouth would not stop. "Do I ... like? I love it!"

"Oh, goodie!" Andrea hugged her, inadvertently slapping her on the side of the head with a menu. "I gotta run and serve some folks, but stop by and see me on the way out, okay? I have a bunch of people wanting your phone number!"

And she was off to fill bellies and quench thirsts.

She let her gaze, once again, wash over the gallery walls featuring her photos. As she stood there, Willow returned and bumped into Melody's leg with her nose.

Together they made their way to one of her usual tables on the patio overlooking the dog yard. A full water dish was tucked beneath the table, and Willow curled up beside it. Two dogs flew through the yard nearby, wrestling over a rope toy. Willow lifted her head, watching them, but Melody wasn't quite comfortable with their aggression. "Stay," she said firmly. Willow lowered her chin back down to the ground.

Yes—progress!

As she sat there taking it all in, Melody swayed between a sense of excitement and another of disbelief. Her quiet escape—photography—had been taken from her one night during the Christmas season, and, frankly, she thought she had put away her camera for good.

But then ... Willow.

She was scrolling through her phone when the gentle clink of a glass on the table caught her attention. She lifted her chin to find a deep orange Aperol Spritz in front of her. "To celebrate," Andrea said, sliding into the open seat across from her. "Hey ... wondering if it's okay to ask you something."

"Sure. What is it?"

Andrea seemed to hesitate. She slid a look out to the yard and back before saying, "This is kind of embarrassing, but, uh, I searched your name on the internet."

Melody laughed nervously. "Why? I'm right here."

"I know, of course, I know. But I was looking for a bio to add to the wall, you know, with the photos?"

Something in Melody's stomach began to twist.

"Well, anyway, I ran across a meme first—quite funny, really. But then it lead to more and I read some things that your ex said. Scott, I mean."

Melody's heart thudded in her chest, the weight of it like a boulder hanging from twine. Of course, *Scott*. No matter how many miles she'd traveled he still managed to cast a shadow over her, though she'd been working hard to slip out from under it as often as possible. Despite the tautness of her muscles, she stayed composed and simply said, "Oh."

Andrea's eyes flew open, and she reached forward and grabbed one of Melody's hands. "I hope you don't think I bought any of his garbage! I doubt anyone does."

Melody blinked. "He's still saying those things about it being my fault the marriage didn't work? About me and ... kids?" Her voice was barely a whisper now.

Andrea nodded, her lip curled in disgust. "Guy's a real piece of work. I'm telling you he's got schmoozy liar written all over his ugly face—no offense; you must've thought he was okay at one time."

She didn't know whether to laugh or cry, but she did

know relief when she felt it flooding through her chest. When Andrea began to speak, she prepared herself for judgment or pity, not such cool solidarity.

"I'm relieved you don't believe him."

"Please," Andrea scoffed. "I've seen enough guys like him to last a lifetime. Just because he's running for mayor doesn't mean he can rewrite history. You're the one who got away from that mess. Good on you."

Melody rubbed her face, painfully aware that her shining moment had, once again, been stolen by Scott. The night she had been taking photos at the hotel was supposed to give her the confidence to, finally, approach the corporate office and ask for a promotion to public relations. Instead, it was the beginning of the end of her marriage to Scott—and she found herself applying for a supervisory position at a quiet inn out of state ...

"I guess I should have confronted him but"—she shrugged—"when my brother called to tell me what Scott was doing and saying, I was so stunned. I chose instead to continue walking away so that I could fully heal."

Andrea smiled. "I applaud you."

"Oh, I don't know. I mean, thank you, but maybe I should have exposed him for who he really is first."

Andrea shrugged. "Maybe. I mean, if it were me, I'd hate for my name to be sullied like that in my own hometown. But at the same time, those people usually make their own press, if you know what I mean."

Melody tilted her head to one side and Andrea slid off the chair and stood next to her. "Your character shines, but guys like that eventually are their own downfall. His character will find him out—I believe that, sister friend."

Willow bumped her nose against Melody's leg and snorted, her tail wagging as if to comfort her. Melody brushed her hand across the puppy's soft fur, feeling the familiar grounding that her faithful companion always brought her.

What a terrible idea it had been to allow Scott free rent in her head all these many months. She knew this with her head and sent him packing as often as possible. But her heart still recoiled with every thought of Scott's rising political ambitions and where they might take him. He was making waves in small-town Ohio. What if that popularity grew? What if she could never fully escape being part of his story?

What if ... what if ... his lies ... his public persona, spread like brine through the sea. She shuddered at the idea of being forever linked to that man and his warped, false version of their time together. Those thoughts haunted her, though she did her best to bury them every time they arose.

"Oh, I almost forgot to give you this," Andrea said, dropping a notepad on the table. "It's that list of people who want to talk to you about your photography."

"Oh!" She glanced at the list, at once grateful to have her mind pulled away from thoughts of Scott, but also intimidated by real people wanting to talk to *her* about something as personal as her photographs. Her emotions had hopped on a seesaw without an exit.

As if on cue, a group of patrons at the next table cooed at Willow, offering her a treat. Melody laughed, happy for the chance to shake off tension. "Careful. She might get a big head over all this attention."

Willow, for her part, happily trotted over to that neighboring table to accept her adoration in the form of a chicken nugget and plenty of pets. Her tail whirred so hard Melody wondered if she might just lift off at any moment.

If only *she* could accept compliments so easily!

"She's got quite the following," one lady shouted. "Between your photos and this girl's charm, your career will take you far!"

Melody thanked her, then leaned back, cradling her spritz, but not taking a sip. Career. If only the woman knew she was a thousand miles away from thoughts of making photography an actual career.

Not that she disliked the direction her real career had taken—she didn't. Though she wondered sometimes if her ideas for improvement would push poor Ethan over the edge one day. ...

She was completely lost in thought now, her mind dipping into the muck of the past and the possibility of the future. Andrea, who had yet to leave the area due to Willow's current reign as queen, stopped next to her. She placed a hand on Melody's shoulder. "Keep doing what you're doing. I'm honored to know you, friend."

The tears took no time in forming and she had to blink them away to keep from drawing attention to herself. As Andrea walked away, Melody found herself lost in thought. Maybe she didn't have to dodge every question about Scott and his nefarious doings. Maybe people would see through him just like Andrea did.

Willow returned, satiated with snacks, and settled at her feet, the steady hum of the cafe her naptime music. Peace had found its way back into Melody's mind and heart. She had escaped once—and, if she had to, she could do it again, though she hoped she never would have to.

Healing had found her. She believed it to her core. From now on, her focus would be her work, her dog, and the life she was continuing to build here in Dragonfly Cove.

On an afternoon walk after the last guest had checked out for the day, Willow stopped to do her business on a dry grassy area in front of a cute little bookstore called Beach Reads.

Melody craned her neck to read the signs on the front of the store. How she had not noticed this cute shop before was anyone's guess. The place struck quintessential coastal vibes with an orange and turquoise exterior. Oh, and those bright yellow French doors called to her—the same color as the inn's front door—along with the sign out front announcing "Dog friendly!" to passersby.

"We definitely have to make a long stop in there soon, Willow." Her pup jumped up, both paws landing on her hips, as if to agree. "Oh, girl, you're growing too fast! Slow down already."

Caring for a growing puppy, getting her vitamin D, and taking up photography again reminded Melody of all the beauty that was still in front of her to see, if she only opened her eyes and paid attention.

She made a mental note to come back to the bookstore with a budget for herself—and for the inn. It so happened that Frank was building and painting a bookshelf for the lobby that would need some shiny new books to fill it soon.

As she and Willow continued on, she turned a corner and spotted the inn, her heart swelling. She hadn't known this place existed just half a year before, and now it had become her home. It might not last forever, but, in her heart, she wished it would.

Willow, too, realized they'd arrived, and she picked up

the pace. Though Willow had become the lobby dog, so to speak, Melody had chosen lately to leave her in the studio with plenty of chicken and sweet potato treats, along with calming music she played on YouTube during especially busy times.

Early fall had come, and, since the inn was experiencing a lull, today would be a good time to reacclimate Willow to her post in the lobby.

When they arrived at the brick driveway, Melody knelt until she was eye-to-eye with Willow. "Remember what I've taught you, girl?" She pointed toward the inn. "You'll go straight up those steps and wait for me on the landing. Can you do it?"

Willow whined and groaned a response, her mouth open, as if acknowledging Melody's instructions and champing at the bit to show off her skills. Melody unhooked the leash and said, "Go."

Without a look back, Willow made a beeline up the front steps, then twirled around in a circle in front of the yellow entry door, before sitting somewhat patiently, tail thumping against the wooden landing, until Melody arrived.

"Good girl!" Melody rubbed Willow's noggin, taking great care to give her plenty of praise. She opened the door. "Go get some water, sweet girl."

Willow padded over to the fresh bowl of water that Maria had set out for her. After several gulps, she crawled into her crate—which Melody noticed was beginning to look small—and curled up into a tight, content ball.

Deep breath in. The lobby smelled of cinnamon and sugar cookies, the chef's welcome gift to today's arrivals. Unable to resist, she grabbed the tongs and placed a cookie in a napkin, noting it was still warm from the oven.

"Mmm ..."

Maria appeared, her eyes drooping. She had taken the early morning shift when the night auditor had to leave for an appointment. By the looks of her, Melody had gotten there just in time.

"Scram. Get out. Go get some sleep."

Maria managed a weary smile. "Those cookies are the bomb. Unfortunately, I ate three of them hoping they'd give me more energy—and all I got was a sugar crash!"

Melody winced. That might have worked in her teens, maybe even her twenties, but those days were over. She slid her gaze to the half-eaten cookie in her hand and frowned, considering whether she'd be fighting off a nap soon too.

Instead, she devoured the rest of it, enjoying every morsel. Maria quickly reviewed the incoming guest list with Melody, then grabbed her purse from behind the desk and headed out with a wave and promise to be back tomorrow.

With Willow quietly sleeping and Maria gone, the lobby seemed awfully quiet again, too quiet for such a sunny day outside where birds sang from swaying palm fronds. Her gaze drifted to the small speaker sitting empty and forlorn on the table near the corner. In her original plans, she would have replaced it by now with something more powerful.

Instead, it continued to sit there, mocking her with its silence.

For weeks, she had been testing the waters, quietly reintroducing subtle changes to the inn's atmosphere, such as earth tone statuary replaced by tabletop decor and layered blankets featuring a fresh palette of soft yellows, whites, and airy blues. She changed out a couple of beige lampshades with crisp white ones etched with waves, and she even talked Frank into hanging a deep-blue pendant light where an old-style, recessed lightbulb had burned out long ago.

The overall effect was modern, yet still warm and inviting. She'd also, of course, updated the check-in system and added the welcome cookies to the process. Ethan had given her the green light early on to use her creativity to win over more guests, albeit reluctantly. And yet, the absence of music continued to gnaw at her.

So ... she decided to try something.

For the past week, as she lay in bed with Willow cuddled on the floor beside her, Melody had carefully curated a playlist of classical crossover tracks, a blend of modern songs and the kind of classical music she had learned that Naomi had loved. She hoped that paying a gentle homage to the inn's previous proprietor would bridge the past with the present—and win Ethan over along the way.

She opened her phone app, and her thumb hovered over the playlist she had created. Soon a delicate, familiar melody filled the lobby.

Willow peeked out of the crate, her forehead lifted until it crumpled. Melody took that as a positive sign that she'd made a good choice. She smiled down at her faithful companion, then leaned an elbow on the desk, and shut her eyes, letting the music seep into her soul.

After two songs had played, seamlessly transitioning one to the other without breaking up the soft vibe, the chime of the front door announced a guest's arrival. Melody straightened and smiled, excited to greet visitors to the inn.

Instead, her eyes landed on Ethan strolling through the front door.

The afternoon sun highlighted the golden whites of his hair. She tried not to allow her gaze to follow that one lock of graying hair that had, apparently, fallen forward when he'd stepped from the drafty outside into the cocoon of the inn's lobby.

He strode toward her, his tall, muscular frame casting a shadow that displayed itself jaggedly across the wood plank floors and the giant, round entry rug. His intelligent blue eyes appeared to flicker with light when their gazes met. Then—just as quickly—they dulled to the inky color she'd noticed in them often before.

His arms seemed to tense, his head tilting slightly toward the adjoining room where so many of the changes Melody had made continued to show off. As the familiar notes of a song began to swirl around the lobby, Ethan turned back to face her, his eyes narrowing.

"What is this?" His voice, though quiet, was laced with a sharp edge that made Melody's heart skip a beat.

"Oh, I think it's that song, "Perfect" ... by Ed Sheeran? The entire song is played with string instruments," she said, deeply aware of how haunting the music sounded under this arrangement. "You didn't have the best reaction to the last playlist, so I thought—"

"No."

A knot formed in her stomach. "I-I don't understand. You don't like the music or—"

"Turn it off," he said, a vague shake in his voice.

She blinked, taken aback by the intensity of his tone. "I heard that, um, Naomi loved classical music, so I tried to choose a style that would, uh, honor her, yet bring some-thing fresh—"

"Didn't you hear me? No. Turn it off."

Melody stared at him. For weeks, she had been careful, stepping lightly around his grief, around the memory of his wife. But he had also warmed to some of the changes she'd brought, and even chided her with a wink and a smile a few weeks ago when she'd bought the hurricane candle lamp. Not to mention the gift he'd given her.

Had she read too much into all that?

His reaction confused her, and, more than that, it reminded her of times in her marriage when Scott's words and actions sent mixed messages. She had promised herself not to cower from her thoughts, nor hide them, like she had done for much of her life.

And yet this wasn't a marriage, but an employment situation. What had she been thinking, treating it like anything but that?

Ethan's face darkened. In her confusion, Melody didn't offer anything more, so he marched over to the speaker and tried to turn it off. She watched him, frozen, as he kept poking around as if trying to find the "off" switch.

Tension crackled in the room, and she said a silent prayer of thanks that no guests had appeared to sense it too. The music that had soothed her nerves now felt more like a taunt. She wanted it off too, and looked around for her phone so she could access the music app.

Willow, sensing the shift in mood, stood up and pressed herself against Melody's leg, her tail tucked between her legs.

Melody opened her mouth to tell Ethan she would turn off the music right away. She pulled up the app, but, in her hurry, she clicked the wrong feature. Ethan stepped closer, his eyes blazing. He stood so close to her she could see the flecks of slate and sky in his eyes.

"You don't get it, Melody," he said, those eyes moving from anger to ... something else. "You think you can just sweep in and make everything better with your photos and your music, but this place is all I have left of her. You can't change that."

"I-I would never." Willow crept out of her crate and started pacing in front of Melody. "I guess I thought this type of music would be a beautiful way to—"

"To what? To remind me that—*that*—song was her favorite? That she sang it to me every chance she got?"

Melody's stomach dropped as she realized that her attempt at change had opened a very tender wound. Sorry wasn't a strong enough word for how she felt. Had she ever known a love like this? Where the notes of a song could be so powerful as to rip open a memory that she both wanted to run to and run from?

The color had drained from Ethan's face. "You don't get to tell me how to grieve."

Willow continued to pace, walking circles around Melody. She let out a soft whimper and Melody gently shushed her, leaving her hand by her side to offer comfort to her dog.

"Ethan, it was never my intention to bring up such memories for you. To be honest, it's awfully quiet in here sometimes."

"What's wrong with quiet?"

She gave him a sad smile. Willow padded to the door, but Melody motioned for her to heel. "Nothing, of course. Quiet is fine, but ..."

"But what?"

She shifted, and licked her lips, thinking, before raising her gaze to meet his. "Is that what you want? For the lobby of the inn to feel somber and sad when guests arrive?"

Willow sent a human-sounding whine into the air.

Ethan stared at her, those eyes swimming with emotion.

They softened, as if her words had found a way into his heart. Maybe he was coming around.

Willow whined again, louder this time, and Melody dropped her gaze to find her pup's ears flattened against her head. Without another warning, her dog squatted down on the circular lobby rug and began to relieve herself, a dark stain quickly spreading across the textile's intricate pattern.

Melody gasped. For too long of a moment, the only other sound in the room was the quiet hum of the music and Willow's soft panting. Dread crept up Melody's spine and she lunged for Willow, knowing full well it was too late. For all she knew, the rug was an heirloom, another beloved memory of his wife.

Ethan's eyes flicked down to the stain, his lips pressing into a thin line. His silence chilled her.

Melody sent Willow into her crate with a word. Then she grabbed a box of tissues and, hands shaking, pulled tissue after tissue from the box, trying to blot the stain. "I'm so sorry. I didn't—she didn't mean to—"

"Get the dog out of here." Ethan's voice, low and cold, had returned.

Melody's head snapped up, her eyes wide. "Ethan, she didn't mean it. She was just—"

"I said get the dog out of here." There was no mistaking the steeliness, the finality, in his tone. "She's not allowed inside the inn anymore."

The wind was knocked right out of her. Willow was her constant companion, her comfort in this new life she was trying to build. The inn had become their shared space, a place where they had both started to find their footing.

She refused to let forming tears fall, the ones that had caught her by surprise. "You can't be serious," she whispered, a noticeable tremor to her voice.

Ethan didn't respond. He simply turned on his heel and walked toward his office, leaving Melody kneeling on the floor with Willow beside her, the soft strains of "Perfect" now playing on loop.

Melody sat there for a moment, staring at the stain, a wad of tissues clenched in her hands. The weight of what had just happened pressed down on her chest, and the line she had crossed lay like a dagger between her hopes and dreams. Maybe Ethan was right. Maybe she had pushed too far.

Deep down, she also knew that what happened just now was about more than a rug or a song. It was about the grief Ethan couldn't let go of, and the changes Melody had been trying to bring. The inn had become a battleground between the past and the future, and, in that moment, Melody realized she was losing the battle.

She stood, her legs unsteady beneath her. "Come on, Willow," she murmured, her voice barely audible. The dog looked up at her with sad eyes, her tail limp. "It's okay, girl. Come on."

Together, they walked out of the lobby, the door closing behind them with a soft click. She sent Maria a quick SOS text, asking her to watch the desk, then stuck her phone into her pocket with no intention of looking at the screen again anytime soon.

Outside, the sun still shone, casting deep golden rays over the inn. But all Melody could feel was the cold silence Ethan had left in his wake.

Chapter Nine

Melody's heart continued to weigh down her chest as she walked along the winding path that led toward the beach. Willow trotted at her side, her tail low, as if sensing Melody's mood. Palm branches rustled, and, not far away, the faint sound of the ocean lapping against the shore attempted to soothe her.

But nothing could at this moment.

Reality blasted her like a stifling summer day on the gulf and she blamed herself. Somehow, in her quest to find acceptance somewhere far from the home she'd left, Melody had made the inn more than a job.

She blinked against the sting of fresh tears. Crying was only a momentary balm. She had cried more tears over the demise of her marriage, over the rejection she'd felt, and, once those tears dried, she vowed never to let Scott hurt her like that again.

But frustration over her mistakes, the assumptions she had made, and the hurt that Ethan's cold words had caused, were too much to hold back. She felt for Ethan too. They'd made a connection at the beach, and again in the garden when Willow had so willingly run to him. She realized now that, because of that, she'd felt free to follow her instincts where the inn was concerned.

Except that Ethan had experienced something so painful, that it ached to know that she had stoked the embers of his grief over Naomi. She had been trying to bring life back to the inn, and Ethan was trying to preserve the life that had been cut short by leaving everything the same.

Melody glanced at Willow, who had come to a stop at a patch of grass near the sidewalk. By the peppy way her tail reached for the sky with each step, Melody knew she'd forgotten all about the drama that had driven them out here.

That brought her a semblance of relief. Her poor dog needn't carry the baggage of guilt around as regularly as Melody did.

"Oh, Willow, I pushed things too far, didn't I?" Gently, she tugged Willow's leash to get her to keep moving. She'd forgotten her training treats, and seemed to have temporary amnesia about what Hank had taught her.

Lost in thought, Melody almost didn't notice the store-front up ahead, *Dogland Pet Store*. Her mind flickered back to the bookstore she had discovered earlier that day, how she longed to go inside and bury her nose in a book. Where was that place again?

She'd never been inside the gaudy Dogland, opting instead to pick up supplies from a smaller, mom-and-pop shop. Something about Dogland always felt off to her, as if dogs were an income-producing enterprise and nothing more.

Willow was content to let her nose run like a vacuum

on the sidewalk in front of the pet store. It was likely she was sniffing the scents of the dogs who had been there before.

As Willow continued inspecting the ground, the door swung open, and Lola marched out.

"Hey there, Lola."

Her friend stopped mid-stride, and her severe expression melted a bit, though fire still lingered there. "You're not planning to shop here, I hope."

"No, we're just ... on a walk."

One of Lola's brows shot up. "Kind of a long way from the inn." She was watching Melody, as if trying to figure out what was behind the poker face she wore.

"Lost track of time."

Lola looked like she wanted to ask more questions, but then she glanced back at Dogland. "Hmm. Okay." She groaned and waved a hand through the air. "That place is awful."

"What do you mean? Did something happen?"

"I learned they're getting their puppies from a puppy mill. A *puppy mill!*" She shook her head.

Melody's stomach churned. She had heard rumors, but hearing it confirmed made her sick. "That's so horrible."

Lola's hands clenched into fists. "I read it in the paper and went in there to let that man have a piece of my mind!" She crossed her arms and screwed up her mouth. "Told him I wouldn't be shopping there anymore, but, spoiler alert, I didn't shop there anyway."

"So nothing to have regret about."

"True."

Melody patted her friend's arm. "You're a good dog mama. Always looking out for the little critters."

Lola unlocked her arms and shrugged. "I doubt it will make any difference, but I just had to say something, you know?" Lola sighed, visibly shaking it off. "You sure you're okay? Did ... did something happen you're not telling me about?"

Melody forced herself to smile, or at least try to, but she imagined her eyes looked like a deer in the headlights and the smile, stiff. She blinked, trying to look and feel more relaxed, but the dam broke. Tears came out and she wiped them away as quickly as she could, embarrassed. "It's just been one of those days, you know?"

"The ex?"

Melody gave her head a tight shake, her mouth closed. "It's getting closer to election day, but, fortunately, I haven't heard much about him." She hoped and prayed she wouldn't.

Lola's expression shifted. "What happened then? Work? Ethan?"

Melody looked away, swallowing. "Oh, I screwed things up."

"Doubtful. Tell me everything."

Melody relayed what had occurred: the music, Ethan's reaction, their sparring, and Willow's accident, which culminated in her being banned from the inn.

Lola's mouth dropped open. "You've got to be kidding me." She bent down and gave Willow some love, rubbing her head and neck vigorously. "Poor thing. You were obviously stressed out by the hoo-mans."

Melody sighed. "Ethan banned my sweet dog—and it's all my fault. She's really kept me sane in this time of upheaval—kudos to Leslie for seeing what I couldn't!" Her shoulders slumped. "I feel kind of silly. True confession: I was never a dog person."

"You don't say."

"Wait. You knew?"

Lola gave her a *sorry* smile. "It's obvious how much you love this sweet creature, and how couldn't you? But you're rather timid around other dogs. It's not a bad thing. Just something I noticed."

"Well, then you'll understand it when I say how much my behavior shocks me. Believe me, I was the first to protest when our hotel chain began accepting dogs overnight." Lola pulled back in surprise. "It's true. One of our front desk clerks called me heartless."

"Well, now, that's silly. Fear doesn't mean someone is heartless." Lola sniffed, indignant. "And you have every right to be upset with Ethan! He can't just—"

She stopped, her eyes narrowing. "Mel, listen to me. You can't let him push you around like this. You and Willow are a package deal, right? You march right back in there and tell him that. Tell him if Willow's out, you're out too."

Melody smiled sadly at her friend's fiery determination. It was classic Lola—bold, brash, and always ready for a fight. But as much as she appreciated the advice, it wasn't that simple. She was at fault here too.

"You're sweet, but maybe I've been wrong about everything. When I interviewed with Ethan, I was at my lowest. Not a lot of fight in me, honestly. He probably thought he was hiring someone who would just keep everything the way it was." She wiped away tears with the pads of two fingers. "Instead, the poor guy got *me*—someone with myriad ideas but not the best judgment."

Lola scoffed, waving her hand dismissively. "Please. You're exactly what that place needs. You've done nothing but improve it since you got there. Look at the photos, the atmosphere—you're bringing life back into that inn, whether Ethan wants to admit it or not."

Melody let out a soft laugh, tinged with sadness. "Maybe. But maybe it's time for me to take myself, my dog, and all my ideas somewhere else. Pretty sure I've worn out our welcome at the inn."

Lola's fierce demeanor faded some. She touched Melody's shoulder, her voice softening. "Look, I get it. It's tough. But you can't just give up. Not after coming all this way and putting your heart into running that old inn in the best way possible."

Melody shrugged, unsure what else she could do at this point. She glanced at Willow, who had now sat quietly at her feet, her eyebrows shifting side to side with worry. "No matter where I end up, sweet Willow, you're coming with me."

She knelt down and pulled her pup close, breathing in the soft pant of puppy breath. Willow licked her face and then sat back on her haunches.

"Shoot," Lola said. "Who needs a man when your dog sends out puppy love vibes like that."

Melody pressed her lips together in a wry smile. She wiped away the last of her tears and stood up again. "I love the inn. Truly, I do. And I thought Ethan and I ..."

Lola's forehead creased. "Hang on a second. Is there something going on with you and Ethan?"

"What? No." Melody shook her head. "I meant I thought we, well, you know, we've been getting along. That's all."

"All right." Lola didn't look convinced, and was silent for a beat. Eventually, she slung her purse over her shoulder and said, "Well, if anyone can figure things out, it's you. You're tougher than you think, Mel. And Willow, well, she's part of the inn now no matter what that grumpy ol' Ethan says."

Melody smiled faintly, her heart a little lighter from the support of her friend. "Thanks, Lola. I appreciate it."

"Anytime." Lola grinned, then gave Melody a gentle nudge. "But, seriously, if you want me to go in there and knock some sense into him, just say the word."

Melody laughed, shaking her head. "I'll figure out a way to handle this one on my own. You've helped me. I promise."

"Suit yourself." She winked. "I'm here if you need backup."

Melody and her pup turned back toward the inn, making a stop at the dog park for Willow to get a nice, long drink of water. As the other pups darted around them, one thing was for sure: Melody had changed. Instead of cowering, she found herself surrounded by little loves whose sole existence, in this moment, revolved around getting pets from her.

Oh, to have such an existence where love is the only requirement. Her mind churned with everything Lola had said. Maybe she had been wrong to push so hard, but Lola was right about one thing: she couldn't give up. This inn, this town, had become her home, and, as much as Ethan's grief loomed over everything, she wasn't ready to walk away from it just yet.

But how could she find a way to stay when she had started to overthink every move she made, every change she conjured up, every upgrade guests seemed to want?

As the sun dipped below the horizon, casting shades of cotton candy and tangerine across the sky, Melody made a silent promise to herself. She wouldn't run. Not yet. There had to be a way to find balance at the inn and to breathe some new life into it without turning up the drama where Ethan was concerned.

She just had to find it.

"And we also have to find a way to get you back in Ethan's good graces, girl."

Willow nudged her leg, as if in agreement, and Melody smiled down at her companion. "Come on, sweet stuff. Let's go home."

As usual, Barks & Brews was packed with patrons and their furry companions lounging around the outdoor seating area. The air hummed with conversation, barks and shushing, and an acoustic guitar's soothing thrum floating through speakers. Melody sat at a high-top with Willow sprawled under the table after running the equivalent of a marathon around the yard. Her nose twitched in the direction of the adjacent table where someone had delivered a basket of fries.

"Not good for doggies," Melody whispered, with a sad little smile. Willow gave up a reluctant sigh and then settled down, sprawling on her side.

Melody's gaze drifted to one of the interior walls, where her photographs were still on display. The longer they stayed up there, the more vulnerable she felt.

"Melody!" a voice called out from behind her.

Melody waved Maria over. She slid onto a stool and dipped a look downward to where Willow lay sprawled. "Hey there, stranger."

"Glad you could make it," Melody said.

"It's fun to see you and your little girl outside of work."

That's pretty much the only way you'll see Willow these days ...

Maria continued. "I've only been in here once, and it was a long time ago." She glanced at a menu. "What's good here?"

"Pretty much everything." Melody pointed out a few of her favorites when a voice called out, stalling her.

Andrea was making her way over, her grin wide. "Hey, my creative friend. How're you doing?"

"Hey, yourself. This is Maria, my coworker and friend."

The two exchanged hellos.

"Aren't Mel's photographs great?" Andrea said. "The customers love them."

Melody smiled, embarrassed.

Maria looked around, her eyes widening. "No way! These are some of your photos, Mel? Why don't you tell a person!"

Andrea cut in. "Yeah, why don't you tell people! You're too humble."

"Well, I don't know if a person can really be *too—*"

Andrea cut her off, looking at Maria. "I've had at least a dozen people ask about commissioning Mel for pet portraits. She's so talented."

Maria was mouthing *pet portraits,* obviously stunned by this news.

A steady flash of heat began its way through Melody and not the good kind. *Stupid hot flashes.* "That's really kind of you to say, Andrea. Not sure about the doggy portraits, but, uh, you never know."

Something sad passed through Maria's expression, but she didn't comment.

Andrea said, "So, Maria, don't you think our Mel here should take some photos of that lovely inn of yours? We could rotate a few of your photos out and put up some of the inn's. I've always admired that place—that yellow door reminds me of lemonade on these hot days we get around here."

"Fantastic idea," Maria said, giving Melody a pointed look. "You should do that."

Andrea slapped the table with menus. "Then it's a plan! I'll be watching for what you come up with. Now, what can I get you ladies?"

They gave their orders and, as Andrea stepped away, Melody's mind wandered to the possibilities. The inn would be a wonderful subject, but she'd prefer to have people—life—in the shots. And dogs would be a whimsical addition too—she winced, the memory of her altercation with Ethan fresh in her mind.

How could she take pictures of the inn when she wasn't even sure she or her dog were all that welcome there?

"Something on your mind?"

"Not really," she said slowly, glancing down at Willow. "The usual, I guess."

"You've been quiet at the inn."

Melody hesitated. She didn't want to dive into the details of her altercation with Ethan or Willow's banishment. Or maybe she already knew? She certainly didn't want this impromptu meetup to turn into a boss-bashing session.

"Can I ask you something personal? I really might be overstepping ..."

Melody sighed. Great. Maria was about to ask about Scott. She figured it would happen sooner or later. She was only surprised it had taken this long. "Spit it out."

"It's just that, well"—she leaned forward— "is there something, I mean, are you and Ethan, you know ..."

Melody stuck out her neck, waiting. When Maria didn't finish, she said, "You know …?"

"Dating?"

Willow popped her head up from her slumber, as if listening.

All Melody could do was blink, the air knocked right out of her. She stared at Maria for a few seconds, then blew a raspberry. "Not what I thought you were going to say."

"Oh, what did you think?"

Melody waved her hands in front of her like windshield wipers. "Nothing. Never mind. Wow. Um, the answer to that is a resounding no." She laughed a little. "But thanks for the laugh."

Maria wore a conciliatory smile now. "Okay, fine. It's just that there's this amazing tension between you two. Never seen anything like it, well, except for my hubs and me."

This … this was not at all where she thought the direction of this conversation would go. Then again, she often found copies of romance novels from Maria's stash, tucked in corners of the inn. It was no wonder her coworker's mind went in that direction.

Truthfully, Melody wasn't looking for romance, especially with someone so obviously still in love with his wife. It was … absurd.

Maria meant well. Sweet of her, really. And a little nosey, too. She dropped her gaze, shaking her head. "I'm sorry to burst that make-believe bubble over your head, Maria, but there is absolutely nothing between Ethan and me. Far from it, actually."

"But don't you find him handsome, even a little bit? I'm right, aren't I?"

The heat in Melody's face was almost too much to bear

and she had the unshakable sense that if she were to glance into a mirror, she'd see a bright red tomato looking back at her.

Maybe one day she'd go looking for love again, but not now—and not with tension so thick between them that she felt she was crushing eggshells with each step when he was near.

Andrea appeared with their drinks, set them down in front of them, and, with a wink, she disappeared again.

"Let's change the subject, shall we?"

Maria laughed. "Okay, you win." She took a sip of her sparkling water with lime. "What do you think of Andrea's suggestion about using the inn as the subject of more photos?"

"Honestly, I think it might rub Ethan the wrong way."

Maria frowned. "Why would it do that?"

"Well, it's just the inn is so personal to him, you know? Based on our last conversation, I just don't think the time is right for me to ask." It may never be right, actually.

"I don't know about that," Maria said. "Maybe if he saw how your photos could bring more attention to the inn, he'd change his mind. You know that revenue has been down the past week, right?"

Melody tilted her head to the side.

"Am I prying here?"

"It's been a little slow lately, but I don't have anything to do with the receipts, really." Melody leaned forward. "Have you heard something about the inn underperforming?"

Maria sat back and put a hand over her mouth.

"Maria?"

"The night auditor mentioned it. Guess I thought it wouldn't be news to you, but you are new around these parts—it's hurricane season, which scares some people."

It made some sense, really. The inn seemed to bustle during the summer, but now, when the weather was beginning to become more tolerable—in her opinion—bookings had dropped off. Maybe it was fear over the weather changing quickly. Or was it something else?

"Oh? When you said something about the last conversation you'd had with Ethan, I thought that meant you'd heard things were a little tight."

Melody held her tongue. She hated to divulge anything about her skirmish with Ethan to Maria, mainly because of how it would look—like she was complaining about the boss to another employee. Though, honestly, Maria was a sweetheart and might have some good insight for her.

Andrea showed up with a couple of plates of food. Dropped napkins and silverware on the table, then sped off to the next table.

Maria took a bite of her burger, chasing it down with a long sip of water. She sat back. "So do you think you'll do it?"

"Photograph the inn?" Melody glanced around, noting some large open spaces on the walls where imposing photos of the inn could really pop.

The idea had its appeal—she loved Sunny Cove Inn, despite her rocky relationship with its owner. And it wouldn't be a bad idea to draw more attention to the place, hurricane season or not. She had been too distracted to realize that, despite summer's wane, the inn should still be full.

But Ethan's reaction to the music had been so visceral, raw. Could she risk stirring up emotions in him again that caused him so much pain?

If it helped the inn? Maybe she should. "I will definitely think about it."

Maria nodded, continuing with her meal, her expression satisfied. Part of Melody felt that everything about this conversation was normal, usual.

The other part questioned everything. Could she really ask Ethan about photographing the inn to then turn around and hang them in a nearby brewery? And would her efforts be met with praise—or disapproval?

Chapter Ten

A few days later, after Melody had walked Willow and settled back into her small studio apartment, she was still trying to push the conversation with Maria out of her mind.

She wasn't sure what confused her more—the fact that the inn was in trouble and she hadn't realized it or that she and Ethan seemed to have a deeper connection.

Both seemed ... crazy to her.

Add to this that she had received two texts from Tommy today:

Dude is climbing in the polls. Woulda been cool to have a bro-in-law as mayor. Just sayin'

Then:

You know I'd go punch him out for what he did to you. If he wasn't always on TV, that's what I'd do.

Okay. If it made Tommy feel better to send her random updates, so be it. She wasn't committing to giving that situation one more brain cell than it deserved, though. Frankly, she had enough to think about.

Melody filled Willow's bowl with fresh food and sank into the worn armchair by the window, a devotional book in her hand, but her thoughts kept drifting back, not to her brother or Scott, but to the inn. To Ethan. To the way his ocean blue eyes turned icy that day when she played Naomi's favorite song.

She sighed and raked a hand through her long locks. Maybe Andrea was right—maybe there was a way to bring more life to the inn, to honor both Naomi's memory and the new chapter Melody was trying to write for herself. But how could she progress when Ethan seemed to want to move forward, but couldn't?

A soft knock on the door startled her. Willow barked, and ran to the door, tail dancing.

Melody glanced at the clock—it was late, past the time most people would drop by unannounced. Maybe one of the guests was in trouble?

She rose, padding to the door, and opened it a crack.

Her heart jolted when she saw Ethan standing there, one hand shoved deep into the front pocket of his jeans, a two-day old shadow stretching across his face.

"Ethan?" Surprise laced her voice. "Is everything all right?"

He cleared his throat, shifting his feet like he was gathering his thoughts, along with the words he wanted to say. Finally, he stood still and their eyes caught. "I'd like to come in and talk to you. May I?"

Melody hesitated, but Willow danced in place, snuffling and snorting at Ethan's feet, and ushering him right on in.

"Sure. Why not." She opened the door wider and stepped aside.

Ethan's downcast face did not bode well for the coming conversation. He strolled in but slowed, hovering near the small kitchen, as if waiting for a table at a coffeeshop to become free.

"You can sit," she offered, motioning to the couch. "If you want."

He nodded, his eyes catching on the reading nook by the window.

"Is that from the lobby?"

"I rescued it, yes. It had been pushed into the hall, so ..."

"So you gave it a home."

A small smile rose to her mouth. "I did." She wondered if he would notice the strategic placement of her throw blanket.

He didn't mention it but brushed his grizzled chin with his fingers and let out a heavy sigh. "Melody."

Her stomach fluttered at the sound of her name coming from his lips.

"I owe you an apology," he continued.

"For what?" She kept her voice even, though her heart raced.

Willow danced around his feet, and his serious expression broke into a grin as he patted her head, eliciting fangirl-like whines.

Melody almost rolled her eyes at the all-out adoration her dog was bestowing on Ethan.

With his hand still massaging Willow's furry little head, Ethan said, "I want to apologize for the way I reacted to the music, and to poor Willow here." He paused, taking a deep breath before continuing. "I've been holding onto Naomi's memory so tightly that I didn't realize how much I was missing all that was going on right in front of me."

Melody's heart softened. The weight of grief, of moments lost, caused his broad shoulders to slump, his sharp eyes to cloud over.

"I didn't mean to hurt you," he said, his voice quieter now. "Or to take my own pain out on Willow. Hearing that song ... well, it brought everything back. Good memories as well as the bad ones. After Naomi died, I didn't handle things well. Everyone quit—except Frank. I was a mess."

He looked her square in the face, his eyes pools of sorrow and hope.

"I'm sorry," Melody said.

He held her gaze. "I didn't know how to run the place without her, and, when I heard your voice on the phone, I knew."

"What ... what did you know?"

"You sounded ... hopeful. And I knew you could pick up where Naomi left off." He shifted, still digging his graceful hands through Willow's fur. "You gave me faith that this place could live on."

Melody swallowed the lump in her throat, feeling the depth of his pain. She had only seen glimpses of his grief before, but now it was laid bare in front of her.

"I never wanted to replace Naomi," she said gently. "You know that, right?"

He closed his eyes briefly, then lifted his chin. "Of course."

He was looking at her now, and she smiled. "I walked in here blindly, really. If only I had known more about your dear Naomi, then I could have honored her better."

Ethan dropped a sigh, hanging his head. He lifted his chin again. "I'm so grateful to you."

Melody blinked in surprise. "Grateful?"

Ethan nodded slowly. "Your thoughtfulness. You were trying to honor Naomi, and I kept getting in the way. The music caught me off guard, really."

"I'm sorry."

He looked up at her, his expression softer now. "Don't be. Naomi loved making people feel welcome. She had this way of making the inn feel like home for everyone who stepped through those doors. And when you started adding your own touches—changing the look of the place, playing that music—it reminded me of how she used to do things. I just ..."

Melody's heart swelled at his words, a mixture of relief and understanding flooding her chest.

"You just ... what?"

He was looking at her now, raw emotion etched into every line of his face along with something else. She searched his face, couldn't take her eyes off him, because what she saw waiting for her was ... hope.

"I was falling for you, Mel. Hard."

Her breathing stilled.

"But when I walked in the doors, to tell you how I felt, I heard Naomi's song playing." He choked up, his eyes filling. Willow seemed to notice and burrowed her head into his lap. "Guilt is a grieving man's closest friend, I regret to say."

"Oh, Ethan."

He swallowed. "I'm so sorry, Mel."

Melody's gaze absorbed the sorrow, the grief, the love, and the pain on Ethan's face, and it took every ounce of courage not to pull him into her arms to offer him comfort. But ...

Did he really just say he had been falling for her? That was one emotion she had not expected.

Or ... had she?

"Remember that late night out on the beach, Mel? You asked me if I couldn't sleep."

"You said you were an early riser."

"I lied."

She stilled.

"Truthfully, I was just ... lonely."

Melody couldn't pull her eyes away from him. She had to fight off the urge to hug him, to tell him that everything was going to be okay from here on out. Instead, she kept her cool and said, "And then you bumped into me."

A twinkle of a smile appeared on his face. "Or maybe it was you who bumped into me."

She opened her mouth to respond, but he stopped her, both palms flashing. "Don't let me out of this so easily. The other night at the inn? Mel, I was out of line," Ethan contin-ued. "And Willow ... she didn't deserve to be banished." A small laugh escaped him, and he took her pup's face in his hands. "I could never banish you. How absurd."

Melody's smile, mixed with tears, grew across her face. "Ethan. It's okay. I understand. Grief is complicated."

He reached his hand out to her now. "So is love." Then, in one fell swoop, Ethan pulled Melody—and Willow—into his arms.

One decision could change the course of a person's life, sometimes in perilous ways.

Scott's campaign for office didn't just fizzle, it imploded one balmy fall evening after he had spent the evening hugging grammas and kissing babies for the local news cameras. Melody had shut out all news of her ex and his underhanded doings, choosing instead to focus on her relationship with Ethan, her upgrades to Sunny Cove Inn, and her efforts to train her beloved dog, Willow.

So it took a text from Jane to alert her to what happened next with her ex-husband's career aspirations:

He kicked a dog! Oh my gosh, Melody, Scott kicked a dog right on camera!

And just like that, Scott's bid for town mayor was over. Oh, he ran all right, had to because his name was already on the ballot, but, the following month, he lost handily. The so-called family man inadvertently showed his true colors once he believed that all the news cameras had gone home.

His character will find him out. Andrea had said those words to her, further cementing Melody's decision not to engage with Scott and his lies—though she sorely had wanted to.

After hearing the news, Melody scooped up Willow, snuggling her close. The pup buried her furry little head into Melody's embrace, as if sensing Mama's need for comfort.

Whenever Melody questioned her ability to care for a puppy, Willow had done what she had from the very start: happily prove that her instincts were always ... perfect.

Epilogue

Not all decisions create havoc. Many cause miracles to happen right here on earth.

Spring was still a month off, and yet the weather on the gulf was perfect for a party.

"Willow, are you ready for cake?" Ethan called out.

Melody spun into the room, taking the sheet cake out of Ethan's arms and setting it out on the large dining table. "There will be no cake for the dog!"

"Aw, come on, sweetheart. It's her birthday," Ethan said in mock dismay. He tilted his chin down to Willow, who watched him in anticipation. "Are you gonna take that from your mama?"

Willow's eyebrows shifted toward Melody who refused to be swayed. She shook her head. "You two are ganging up on me. I won't have it!" She laughed, patted Willow's head, and smacked a kiss on Ethan's cheek. "Don't worry, either of you. I have ordered doggy cupcakes from Sticky Buns."

Willow sat, rump down, watching the volley of conversation, her chin turning left to right to left again and back.

"Yum." Ethan laughed. He poked his fists into his

sides. "Well, girl, I guess we're going to have to earn our keep around here if we're going to eat ribs and cupcakes later."

Melody tsked. "Don't worry that handsome head of yours—I ordered cinnamon rolls for the rest of us."

Willow let out a brief, high-pitched "hmm?" and both Melody and Ethan cracked up. Ethan shook his head. "Man, sometimes I really think she's—"

"Hoo-man, as Lola would say?"

"Yup."

Melody laughed, too, and tried to pass by Ethan on her way back to the kitchen to grab the cutlery for their guests who would be arriving soon. But he stopped her, pulling her close.

"Hey," he said.

She tilted her chin up, her gaze taking in the sparkle of his azure eyes as they held hers. "Hey, yourself."

"Have I told you lately how happy I am that you answered that want ad last year?"

Melody slid her arms around Ethan's waist. "You may have mentioned it a time or two."

"Hmm. Well, I'm saying it again." He bent slightly to give her a soft kiss on the lips. "I'm really, really, *really* glad you took over my inn—and my life."

"Oh, is that the way you see it? I 'took over?'"

His face split into a grin. Willow, sensing that Ethan could use some help, stood on her hind legs and pressed her paws into his hip. Ethan put an arm around the dog. "I'd say this is some serious agreement from our Willow, wouldn't you say so, girl?"

Willow let out a cross between a whine and a groan that, while open to interpretation, sounded awfully like a conspiratorial agreement with Ethan.

Melody laughed and rubbed Willow's head playfully. "You!"

"Hey there, break it up you three! We have a party to throw." Maria rolled into the room with a stack of plates and napkins. She set them down and looked around the room. "Everyone is going to love these photographs of the inn, and of Willow and the rest of us, Melody. Honestly, the way the light hits them all, especially in this room, well, you outdid yourself."

"I'll say she did!" Lola stepped into the lobby with Henry scampering next to her until she spotted Willow and began chasing her through the dining room.

Melody laughed at the spectacle of two best pals running amok, then gave her friend a hug. "Thanks for all the encouragement you gave me."

Lola put a hand to her chest and sent a proud look up toward the heavens. "To think, I knew you *when*."

Melody slid a gaze over the framed photos on the walls of the dining room, the same images that had graced the walls of Barks & Brews for the past six or so months. They'd ignited new interest in Sunny Cove Inn, and she could not have been more pleased.

A commotion from behind caught their attention. Frank bumbled his way in from the kitchen area, struggling with a large bouquet of balloons that trapped him in the doorway. Lola sprang forward, red boots clicking down the hall. "Here, let me help you with those, Mr. Fix-It!"

Melody laughed as the two became twisted up in the bouquet. She was about to step in to help when a sixty-something woman with spiky white hair stepped into the lobby with a bright-blonde Labrador puppy who looked remarkably like Willow.

Melody greeted her. "Hi there."

"I heard there's a party here today," the woman said.

"That's right," Melody said. In fact, Willow's birthday party and the inn's open house was about to start. "Welcome!"

The woman stuck out a hand. "I'm Dorothy, and this is Sadie."

Melody bent down to greet Sadie, offering her hand, but Willow pushed her way into the mix, landing both paws in front of Sadie, daring her to play. Melody laughed and looked up at Dorothy. "I've seen you walking by here. Is it possible Sadie is one of Leslie's puppies?"

"Yes, ma'am. These two girls are sisters! I only figured it out recently when I saw you running through some drills with your pup outside—Sadie showed that same kind of stubbornness at first."

Melody peeled a look upward at Ethan who playfully shushed her with a forefinger to his lips. So she was a back-slider when it came to training her pup? Willow would come around, eventually. Right?

Dorothy continued. "I can help you train this little gal, if you'd like. I've raised nineteen children, so I've got plenty of tricks up my sleeve!"

Melody grinned. "Wow. I bet you do. May just take you up on that, Dorothy, but, for now, come on in and take a look around. We're happy to have you."

Two hours later, the inn had welcomed guests from all over town, well-wishers who bestowed birthday wishes on Willow and renewed interest in the inn with the yellow door. Guests oohed and aahed over the airy feel of the old place and the photographs on the wall that captured moments in time that could be savored for years to come.

To think, a year earlier, Melody had hung up her camera for good, no thought of ever using it to take a photo again. And then along came Willow, Ethan—and the inn—and the rest?

Well, let's just say, the rest was history and Melody felt gloriously unleashed to use her talents—for good.

If you enjoyed Melody and Willow's story, you'll want to read about Dorothy and her sweet puppy, Sadie in TEACHER'S PET, the next book in the Dragonfly Cove Dog Park Series.

Here's more about it:

Welcome to the dog-friendly town of Dragonfly Cove, where you'll find plenty of heartwarming moments that blend canine companionship into the everyday lives of ordinary people, to create extraordinary stories. If you loved books like Wish Me Home by Kay Bratt, the Hometown Harbor series by Tammy L. Grace, and the Guiding Emily series by Barbara Hinske, you will enjoy the books in the bestselling Dragonfly Cove Dog Park series—heartwarming stories of the dogs who rescue us!

Teacher's Pet, by David Johnson, is the eighth book in the Dragonfly Cove Dog Park series.

Sadie is a bright-blonde Labrador puppy, content and happy to spend her days sleeping, eating, and playing with her seven siblings. But her world is turned upside down when she's given to the oldest human she has ever met. Confused at first, she soon decides she's supposed to watch out and take care of the human named Dorothy who proves to be quite a handful.

Dorothy is a sixty-six-year-old retired schoolteacher from Nashville, Tennessee, who has never been married but has nineteen children. At least, that's what she tells everyone.

Dorothy and Sadie quickly bond with each other, leaving both feeling content. Things change, though, when Dorothy receives an unexpected letter in the mail, a letter she refuses to open for over a week because it's from Harliss Abernathy, the man who left her standing at the altar fifty years ago.

In the midst of trying to decide what to do about the letter, a young woman, Hope Rodriguez, shows up with an ulterior motive. Try as she might, Dorothy tries to point Hope in a direction that will lead her away from her seedy-looking boyfriend, not knowing she's putting herself at risk by doing so.

Will she open the letter? What does it say?

Will Hope Rodriguez harm Dorothy?

How will Sadie help Dorothy navigate these prickly situations?

Hurry and read *Teacher's Pet* and be entertained by this warm-hearted drama.

The Dragonfly Cove Dog Park series is perfect for fans of women's fiction who love stories that are as heartwarming as they are entertaining.

★ Don't miss any of the Dragonfly Cove books! Download them all today! ★

Book 1: Pick of the Litter
Book 2: Collar Me Crazy by Kay Bratt
Book 3: Hearts Unleashed by Tammy L. Grace

Book 4: Back in the Pack by Barbara Hinske
Book 5: Loyal & True by Ev Bishop
Book 6: Coming Home to Heel by Jodi Allen Brice
Book 7: Unleashed Melody by Julie Carobini
Book 8: Teacher's Pet by David Johnson
Book 9: A New Leash on Life by Patricia Sands

Before you go ...

Since you're a dog lover, you'll also want to pick up Julie's novel, *Reunion in Saltwater Beach*, about a big-city lawyer, the small-town beach girl who broke his heart, and a pup named Olive who needs a family 🖤

Acknowledgments

Thank you, readers, for visiting the town of Dragonfly Cove in this latest installment of our dog park series. What a labor of love to join with so many lovely authors to create a special story world for pups to mingle and readers to enjoy!

If you enjoyed *Unleashed Melody*, I'd be honored if you would leave a review on your favorite book site, such as Goodreads, BookBub, etc.

I would also like to thank my sweet husband, Dan, and our adult kids, Matt, Angie, and Emma, for all your support. Thanks also to Mom for telling all your church friends about my books! And a special shout out to Dancer the Dog, who has given me hours of inspiration.

I am grateful to Dione Benson, for your valuable editing service, Elizabeth Mackay for the beautiful cover, and Diana Lesire Brandmeyer for your thoughtful feedback.

Catch up with me on Instagram and Facebook, where I talk about life on the coast, my seaside books, and, of course, my beach dog, Dancer. And stop by my website to grab a free copy of Dreaming of You, a novella in my popular Sea Glass Inn series.

Cheers,

Julie

About the Author

JULIE CAROBINI is the award-winning author of over two dozen beach-themed novels. Her books feature captivating heroines, endearing heroes, and a cast of quirky friends, all bound together by the secrets they hold. Her bestselling titles include *Walking on Sea Glass, Runaway Tide,* and *Reunion in Saltwater Beach.* Julie has received awards for writing and editing from The National League of American Pen Women and ACFW, and she is a double finalist for the ACFW Carol Award. She is the mother of three young adults and lives on the California coast with her husband, Dan, and their rescue pup, Dancer.

Please visit her at
www.juliecarobini.com